T0120876

BRANCH'S DESTINY

BRANCH'S DESTINY

Richard M Beloin MD

Copyright © 2020 by Richard M Beloin MD.

ISBN: Softcover   978-1-6641-3799-8
               eBook   978-1-6641-3800-1

All rights reserved. No part of this book may be reproduced or transmitted in any form or by any means, electronic or mechanical, including photocopying, recording, or by any information storage and retrieval system, without permission in writing from the copyright owner.

This is a work of fiction. Names, characters, places and incidents either are the product of the author's imagination or are used fictitiously, and any resemblance to any actual persons, living or dead, events, or locales is entirely coincidental.

Any people depicted in stock imagery provided by Getty Images are models, and such images are being used for illustrative purposes only.
Certain stock imagery © Getty Images.

Print information available on the last page.

Rev. date: 10/23/2020

To order additional copies of this book, contact:
Xlibris
844-714-8691
www.Xlibris.com
Orders@Xlibris.com
821379

Contents

Dedication

I dedicate this book to two long standing horse loving friends

Jerry and Lynn

BOOK ONE
Branch and Gail

CHAPTER 1

Branch's Beginning

Branch, son of Alden and Flora West, was born in 1871 in Durango, Colorado. His father was one of two foremen in the Durango Hammer Mill and Smelter, while his mom worked at the Wallace Mercantile—owned by Efrain and Agatha Wallace. Branch had two older brothers, Lou who was four years older and Kip being six years ahead of Branch.

Family life was a stable affair with both parents working and the three boys having access to the town's friends, it's many fishing locations, and access to a 22 rifle for plinking or squirrel/rabbit hunting. Suddenly, when Branch hit age 12, the family experienced its first disruption—an event that Branch never saw coming.

The senior West with his connection at the smelter, and a mine that the smelter owned, arranged for his two oldest sons to go to work in the mine. Lou and Kip were happy with the chance to make some money. After working all day in the mine, neither boys wanted to do anything with Branch after their late supper.

Branch tried to make new routines with the local kids, but Branch was not enthused with the results. Fortunately, for his 13th birthday, Branch got a real cowboy gun in 22 caliber. To pay for his ammunition which cost two bits for a box of 50 rounds, he went to work for Sam Monroe at his gun shop. Every day after school and all of Saturday, Branch would run errands, clean guns, help buffing gun parts to perform action jobs. In return, he got all the ammo he needed. For weeks he practiced shooting his pistol and finally realized two important facts. First, he had the natural ability of pointing his pistol at the target and hitting it without aiming. Secondly, he would never be a fast draw gunfighter. Because of an old sports injury, he could not grip the gun handle and snatch it out of the holster with any significant speed, as well as not having enough strength to cock the hammer with his deformed thumb.

One Saturday, Branch came to work early. Stepping in the shop, Branch took the opportunity to speak with Sam before the shop opened. "My Pa wants me to try working in the mine. Lou is making 50 cents a day and Kip makes more at 75 cents." Sam knew this day would come and quickly added, "it's time for me to pay you and I would gladly pay you 50 cents a day on Saturday and another 50 cents for after schoolwork hours."

"Well, the reality is that I'm graduating from high school in a month since I started school early. At age 15, I can now be hired as an apprentice in the mine, and that is what my Pa wants me to do." "Well, since you know the gun trade, if it don't work out in the mine, come and see me. I'll hire you full time and match or better the mine's wages."

*

The first day in the mine was a revelation. As they were walking in the entrance, Branch felt the tunnel walls and ceiling close in on him. The deeper he went in, the faster his heart would race, the more he was sweating and finally kept saying he couldn't breathe. The job foreman recognized the problem and sent his men ahead so he could talk to Branch.

"What you're experiencing son is the fear these walls and ceilings will close in and crush you. Well, that's not going to happen. The walls and ceilings are shored up with 6X6 inch timber. It would take an earthquake to cause a collapse. So, sit here, look around, talk to yourself, keep saying that you can always run out of the adit tunnel, convince yourself that there is plenty of room and air to breathe. When you're settled down, come and join us. You'll take over control, like all the men have done when first in the mine."

The foreman assigned Branch to pick up the loose fallen rock tailings that interfered with the minecart steel wheels. He had several wheelbarrows to fill during the 500-foot trek to the outside, but at least he was able to catch a full breath every time he reached the open air. After dumping the useless tailings, he reentered the dreaded adit to repeat his clean up job. Several weeks passed as a new young man took over his job and Branch took a job cleaning up after the dynamite blasts. The mine was not modernized with a compressed air mucker, so the blasting debris had to be picked up manually or by shovel, and loaded in the railed minecarts.

One day, the earth shook, and it wasn't caused by dynamite. Everyone went quiet as they heard a massive cave-in. Everyone ran down the adit to find it completely plugged. The cave-in was massive and the only miner absent was the new boy who had replaced Branch. The question was whether he was ahead or under the fallen dirt and rocks.

Realizing the miners were trapped, Branch said, "we're all going to run out of air and die!" Kip responded, "not likely little brother. We have a 3X3 foot air shaft with a cage hoisted up by a windlass. Since, you're the youngest man here, you get to go first."

Branch was helped into the cage and when the door was closed and secured, his heart started racing and true panic followed. When Kip pulled the up-rope, Branch was lifted up the 150 feet to the outside world. Every upwards foot was complicated by falling dirt from the loosened 4X4 timbers used to build the shaft. In total darkness and totally helpless, Branch then made a promise to God. "If you get me out of this hell hole, I will dedicate years of my life to do your good will!" Suddenly, darkness started to dissipate and in seconds, the cage erupted in the high noon sun.

Branch jumped out of the cage, jumped face down on the ground and only said for no one to hear, "Lord, my promise is my word, once I figure how to achieve this goal." For the remainder of the day, everyman was pulled out of the mine thru the cage in the air shaft. The boy working the adit tunnel was not found and presumed under the rubble. Before walking home, Branch went to the office, quit his job, drew his pay and never looked back.

*

It took two days for Branch to settle his nerves. Meeting up with Sam Monroe, he gladly took the job as Sam's assistant at $5 a week. After explaining his dilemma of not ever being a fast draw, he asked Sam how he could use a firearm to defend himself if he ever became a lawman. Sam understood the situation and agreed to start working on the solution.

Weeks went by, and Branch learned the trade. He started breaking down pistols and rifles and rebuilding them. He could see in some strange dimensions how one tiny part would activate the next part and so, on and on, and on, till the last part, the firing pin, made the gun go bang. Two months later, unknown to him, Sam was finishing the modifications to two firearms specifically altered for Branch.

One Sunday afternoon, Branch was invited to Sam's private range behind the gun shop. "As you know, I've been working on a solution for your right hand and right arm weakness. You need a primary firearm and a backup firearm whose end result is based on your innate ability to point and shoot. The primary weapon is a lever action 12-gauge shotgun just produced by Winchester and it's the model 1887."

"I took a production weapon and modified it to make it a gunfighting firearm. Here are the external changes. The barrel is only 14 inches and the forearm was cut to be one inch shorter than the barrel. The end of the forearm has been rounded for smoothness and the magazine tube under the barrel holds three shells. The shoulder stock has been partially cut off. What remains is the pistol grip bootleg and about 1.5 inches of the cheek rest—now this is called a 'mare's leg.' The cut off end has been sealed with a curved smooth steel plate. The last change was adding an extension spur on the lever's trigger guard—more on this adaptation in a minute."

Branch was amazed at what he saw. "Now for the internal changes. The original lever traveled over a long throw of about 8 inches, making speed shooting impossible. I shortened this swing to 3 inches. Now when you close the lever, this spur in the trigger guard automatically engages the trigger and fires the weapon—and every time you cycle the action, as soon as you close the lever, it fires without you pulling the trigger. Also the hammer has a reduced spring which you can pull with your bad thumb. Let me demonstrate!"

Sam adds three shells in the lower magazine tube, a shell in the chamber, closes the lever, and then engages the automatic spur in the trigger guard. Then before placing the loaded firearm in its special holster, you carefully de-cock the hammer just like you do with any single action pistol. Then hook the mare's leg in its special holster which I'll explain after the demo."

Without any warning, Sam detaches the mare's leg from its holster, anchors the butt plate on his holster belt in front of the holster, pulls the hammer back, pulls the trigger, and quickly cycles the lever three times. The result was BANG-BANG-BANG-BANG. Branch was hopping around on one leg, the smoke was so thick you could barely see your hand, his eyes were as big as tin cups, and his ears started buzzing from the muzzle blast. Sam had a grin from ear to ear and said, "gosh, I love this baby, it really is a gatling gun in your hands, and can you imagine what four loads of OO Buckshot will cause in human devastation?"

"Unbelievable, I want it, no I need it. Now please explain how this holster works?" "This is a hip strap that is the integral part of the three- inch belt. The back-belt loops hold 45 caliber and 12-gauge shells. Instead of a cup type standard holster, this hip strap has a C shaped clamp that attaches to the receiver just above the wood forearm. The tip of the hip strap has a cup with a center pin that holds the barrel tip from falling out. You extract the shotgun by grabbing the pistol bootleg and pushing it forward to release its hold on the receiver. In one full motion you swing the mare's leg forward, cock it, anchor the butt plate on your 3-inch belt, pull the trigger, and work the lever as fast as you can. Just remember, once a loaded gun goes on your clip-on holster, the hammer should be down on the half-cock position and the automatic spur set. Now try it."

Branch loaded up, did everything Sam had done and started. He first fired by pulling the trigger and then started working the lever with all his might. As fast as he worked the action front to back, the shotgun fired. He repeated the process and with four tin cans at 12 yards he pulverized all four with his natural ability to point and shoot. The only requirement to handle recoil was the need for the steel butt plate to be anchored on his 3-inch belt, and his left hand secured on the forearm.

"Thank you, Sam Monroe, I'll take it. How much?"

"Hey, we ain't done yet. You need a backup gun since you only have four shots out of your mare's leg. What do you do if you are attacked by six outlaws?"

"Yes, I see your point, but knowing you, I'm sure you have an answer, heh?"

"Well of course. Slip this holster to the left of your rig's belt buckle and slip this pistol in the holster. Notice how the pistol lays almost 45 degrees, side to side, in the cross-draw holster instead of the standard up and down position. This 45° side to side pistol lay allows you to pull it out without lifting it up."

"That's a great help but it doesn't resolve the issue of cocking the pistol's hammer with my bad thumb."

"Let me show you something new. He takes the pistol, loads it, then puts his left hand in his pocket, and proceeds, with his right hand, to fire six rounds out of the pistol. "What the heck, what is that thing?""

"This is a new Colt Model 1878 in 44-40 caliber. It is a double action pistol, not a single action like the Colt Peacemaker. You don't have to pull the hammer back, just pull the trigger. Now I performed an action job on the internal parts and made some changes to make it more durable. This will be your back up gun. Once your mare's leg is out of ammo, hold it by the forearm with your left hand and pull your backup gun out with your right hand. Now you'll need plenty of practice before you're ready to go against outlaw gunfighters."

"Sam, I'm overwhelmed, I want these guns and before I get a loan, I need to have a price. How much?"

"The price is a commitment; I want you to stay and work in my shop till your 18ᵗʰ birthday. I will increase your wages to $1.50 a day and charge you ammo at my cost. If you reload ammo, I will supply the components and the reloading tools, you supply the labor, and we share 50/50 the loaded rounds. Six months before your 18ᵗʰ birthday I will hire your replacement so you can train him. On your birthday, those guns are yours and I know you will leave to become a lawman or a bounty hunter."

"Sam, that is a deal and I promise to stay till I'm 18. I also accept the challenge to reload our ammo, both pistol and shotgun."

*

For the next two and a half years, Branch applied himself to working productively at the gun shop, the shooting range, and the reloading bench. He had few social interactions with the fairer sex and his perpetual pastime was to practice the draw and shooting of both his firearms. Most of the time, his emphasis was on the lever action shotgun.

Over time, he documented his reaction time. In the first days, he could draw his mare's leg, shoot four tin cans at 25 feet, and hold his mare's leg with the left hand as he pulled out his DA(double action) pistol, and fired one round at the fifth tin can and hit it. This was all done with the point and shoot method without aiming and in 19 seconds. After a year and a half of daily practice, the same feat was now accomplished in 5 seconds.

Branch worked 8 hours a day in the gun shop. In no time, there wasn't a job he could not do. Selling firearms required a free-flowing knowledge of the different models on display from pistols to rifles to shotguns. Any negotiation of prices other than the tagged price was done by Sam. Ninety percent of sold firearms were sold as tagged and Branch took care of the sale himself. Branch became familiar with the dismantling of any firearm in general use. Repairing them was a simple task and Sam gladly let him at the repairs. When business was slow, Branch would sit at the reloading bench and pump out loaded rounds for sale in the shop—he didn't share in the reloads done during work hours.

Reloading at home was a 50/50 proposition—half reloads to Sam and half to Branch Sam had purchased two reloading presses—one for the shop and one for Branch's home. These universal presses converted from paper shotgun shells to brass pistol/rifle cartridges. The press was a single stage and Branch would prepare 100 casings, and add 100 new primers. The next step was to add FFF Black powder while using a brass scoop to prevent a sparking explosion. The 45 and 44-40 brass pistol/rifle cartridges would be charged with 40 grains of FFF powder as the shotgun shells were charged with 65 grains of FFF powder. Then the brass cartridges would have a bullet added while the shotgun casings would have a lubricated paperboard wad over the powder and nine 0.33-inch pellets added over the wad. The final step was crimping the cartridge onto the lead bullet, or crimping the paper cartridge over the lead pellets.

Time moved on and Sam found a suitable worker. Branch took months to train him and being quite astute, he quickly learned the trade. As his 18th birthday was a week away, the town sheriff had an accident and broke his leg. Branch's dad saw an opportunity to push his son into lawman work which was certainly safer than bounty hunting. Branch agreed to an interview with Sheriff Watson.

That infamous morning, while driving the home buggy, he dropped his mom off to work at the Wallace Mercantile. As she was stepping down, Efrain Wallace came running out and said, "Branch, please get Doc Wilson and Sheriff Watson, we've been robbed, and Agatha was pistol whipped." "I'll get the doc, but the sheriff is useless in bed with his full-length leg cast."

Arriving with the doc, Branch asked Efrain what happened. "Three scruffy miscreants jumped us and demanded I open the safe. I refused since it contained a week's income. They reacted by pistol whipping poor Agatha. I nearly died to see her in so much pain, so I opened the safe and they robbed us of almost $600." "Did you see which direction they took?" "Yes, they went east in the mountains." "Could you identify them if you saw a wanted poster on them?" "Yes, I know I could." "Then let's go to the sheriff's office and go thru the wanted posters."

While Efrain was checking out the posters, Branch explained what had just happened to the sheriff. Sheriff Watson was disgusted at not being able to go after the thieves. Branch finally said, "I'll go after them and bring them back with Efrain's money." Efrain stepped up and handed Branch three wanted posters. The three were wanted dead or alive for several murders during bank robberies in New Mexico. Sheriff Watson said, "All three have $1,000 rewards which means they are violent and dangerous killers. Are you sure you want to tackle them; it sounds like they are cases for US Marshals?" "By the time they get here the trail will be cold, if they ever come. No, I'm gearing up with supplies and going after them."

*

The tracks were hard to follow since the outlaws were not pushing their horses and making deeper tracks. They must have known that this mercantile heist, in the early morning, was easy cash since the sheriff was out of commission and the mercantile owners were elderly. Branch kept looking at the outlaw faces and remembering their names: Mitch Henderson, Weldon Fowler and Titus Wheeler. When darkness came, Branch set up camp. He was new at this and decided to build a fire to prepare a hot meal, ward off the cold air, and tempt the outlaws to visit his camp during the night. Branch's rationale was simple, as he said to no one, "let the enemy come to me instead of me walking solo into an enemy camp!"

By the time he finished his canned beef stew and beans, he heard riders entering his camp. Standing at the ready, he cocked the mare's hammer and activated the automatic spur. "Hello, the camp. Can we light down, we'd like some of that coffee that's brewing." "Sure, come on in. Where you heading?" "We're on our way to Durango." As the three tied their horse's reins to some pine branches and started walking towards the fire, Branch yelled, "STOP RIGHT THERE."

"Friendly visitors don't enter an unknown camp after nightfall, and they certainly don't enter with their hammer loops off their pistols. So, it looks like you are here for nefarious reasons. You figured you could waylay me, steel my guns, horse, supplies and my money. Well, let me tell you this, I've been tracking you all day for that robbery in Durango. Now to my pleasant surprise, I have three wanted posters on you killers, and you're worth $3,000 to me. So, you're under arrest for bank robbery and murder—PUT YOUR HANDS UP OR DRAW"

Branch saw himself enter into a strange trance. He could see the outlaws in slow motion. The outlaws were shocked when they realized they had walked into the predator's lair. Branch saw the outlaw's fine details in their facial expression, could even see the fine hairs in their nostrils move with every breath. Suddenly he saw their pupils nearly close up as they moved their gun arm shoulders about and went for their guns. At that exact moment, Branch released the mare's wrath and before any pistol was out of their holsters, all three outlaws were blown off their feet and tossed into the bushes.

Time seemed to freeze till Branch eventually came out of his trance and returned to reality. The first thing he did was to reload his mare's leg. Then he checked the three bodies to make sure they were dead. Finally, he emptied the outlaw's pockets and brought their saddlebags to the fire. There he had his first cup of coffee as he went thru their belongings. The inventory yielded, one 50X binocular, one sewing kit, a bottle of carbolic acid, one jackknife, three boxes of 44-40 ammo and one box of 41 caliber ammo with a brand-new derringer still in the box. Cash amounted to $3,941.

The next morning he managed to load and secure all three outlaws onto their horses. Trailing the three outlaw horses, he arrived in town by 2PM. At the sheriff's office, he learned that the bounty had already been paid to Western Union and the three telegraph vouchers would arrive tomorrow. For the rest of the day, he disposed of the three Win 73 rifles and three Colt Peacemakers for $180. Sam explained that each Colt pistol was worth $25 with gunbelt, and the Win 73 rifles were worth $35 each.

Selling outlaw horses was not as clear-cut as selling firearms. The well-known hostler explained, "outlaw horses are always the best quality you'll ever find in durable mounts. First of all, you need a clearance from the local lawman that these horses are cleared for public sale. Then you need to dicker with the livery man for a good price. In general, if you get $60 a horse and $30 for saddle and tack, you got a good pay. Now in this case, I'll take those two outlaw horses and the one you rode on. I cannot take that one outlaw horse, because you need it. It is a 17-hand muscular 5-year-old Chestnut gelding with a well-made light saddle. He is calm and gentle and will make you a trail horse for years. For the other three I'll give you $240." "Deal! But Chester needs four new shoes for that price, heh?" "Yes, deal."

*

The next day, the telegraph vouchers totaling $3,000 arrived and Branch opened an account in the Community Bank with a $5,000 deposit. He chose this bank over Wells Fargo or 1st National because in his travels he would often be in small towns where the Community Bank system was more common than the big state and regional banks. After keeping $400 in cash, he gave Efrain $800. Agatha spoke up, "but that's $200 over our loss." "The extra money is to pay for your medical bills and to compensate you for the aggravation this heist caused you."

For the next two days, Branch got geared up for trail work. He bought an 8X scoped Win 76 rifle in 45-70 with a scabbard. He also bought a standard saddlebag for personal items and extra clothing; and an extra-large saddle bag for cooking utensils and vittles. Bulky items such as a rain slicker, winter coat, and tarp were placed in a canvas bag and secured on top of the saddlebags.

During these two days, he took out Chester several times to make sure he gave a smooth ride and that they were compatible in character. He also went to the range and sighted in the rifle at 100-200-300-400 yards and memorized the scope settings for each yardage. With everything ready, he invited Sheriff Watson to dinner at Walt's diner, next door to the sheriff's office. Sheriff Watson was just getting use to walking with crutches but managed to get to the diner by himself.

While waiting for their order, the sheriff asked why he was invited to this meeting. "Well, you see, I'm going on the bounty hunting trail, and I just don't know where to start. It seems fruitless to start traveling from town to town without a destination or an outlaw to chase. So, I wondered if you could direct me into the right path."

The most productive way is to take advantage of the lawman hot line on the telegraph. Lawmen report of the criminal activities in their town and the direction the outlaws took during their escape. Or, they put out a request for some assistance in dealing with a specific situation or gang. Now take right now as an example. There is very little criminal activity around the Durango area and a hundred miles in any direction. However, 300 miles from here in La Junta, all hell has broken out." "Wow, that will take me a week to get there if I push my horse and don't get waylaid."

"Wrong. This is 1888 and we have railroads. It's an eleven-hour ride to La Junta with passenger exchange stops in Antonito and Walsenburg as well as coal and water stops every +- 35 miles. If you choose to take this caper, then I will notify Sheriff McBride of your arrival and my recommendation on your ability to take care of the problem."

"Unless, I'm getting ahead of myself, if I resolve the issue in La Junta, then hopefully Sheriff McBride will send me to another town with a problem and hopefully will include his recommendation to the next lawman." "You got the gist of it."

They then put off their discussion till they finished their meal of roast beef, baked potato, fresh cucumbers and hot corn off the cob. Over coffee, Sheriff Watson had several recommendations to share. "First of all, when confronting outlaws, remember that most are killers. If one goes for a gun, it's time to kill or be killed. Secondly, don't be foolish and try to save the life of a killer by putting your life in danger. Third, when outnumbered, you need to even the odds. Your lever shotgun helps, but so does a long-range scoped rifle or dynamite. Fourth, whenever possible wait for the outlaws to come to you where you have better control of their behavior. Fifth, notoriety is not your best friend. Never do anything to self-aggrandize your prowess with firearms. It won't take long to inherit a moniker for using that altered lever action shotgun. Lastly, there is a new method being used to demoralize the enemy and disable selected victims. That is called jungle warfare and I know that Efrain has added five books on bounty hunting methods, including jungle warfare, to your order. I have seen these books by Swanson, Harnel, Adams, McWain and Harrison. They will make great reading while traveling on trains all over the state."

As they were parting, Sheriff Watson asked, "why are you going on this bounty hunting trail, wouldn't it be safer to work for me as my deputy than to risk your life every day for big money?"

"I'm not doing it for money, I'm doing it to fulfill a promise I made three years ago to a higher power. I guess I'm on a mission, to take out of humanity, evil men that cause so much pain, grief, and sadness."

"Hey, I'm not the most educated man in town but I'm certainly not a yokel. Unless I'm mistaken, that kind of mission means that you are now a 'Paladin,' heh?"

***

CHAPTER 2

Experience the Hard Way

Branch approached the ticket counter and asked for the price of a ticket to La Junta. The clerk said, "that'll be 320 miles at 4 cents a mile or $12.80. Options include: two full meals, one snack, and unlimited coffee for $3, a pullman berth for $2, and a horse tag with hay every four hours for $2.50." "Fine, I'll take a ticket with all three options plus a bait of oats for the horse twice on the trip." "Ok, that's an extra 50 cents. The total comes to $20.80." "Didn't you forget to charge me for the horse's water?" "No sir, that's free!"

The train took off at 5PM. Since this was Branch's first train ride, it took a while to get use to the clackety-clack of the steel wheels hitting the rail unions as it took some time to adapt to the swaying motion of the passenger car. By 6PM a full supper was served to the paying customers. A full meal of pan-fried chicken with fried onions, relish and mashed potatoes. The apple pie was a real treat. After the meal, Branch settled down with one of the bounty hunting books. Before he opened the book, he spent some time looking at the passengers. Of the 23 in Branch's car, only two looked suspicious. They looked nervous for no reason, were well healed with their gunfighter rigs and fancy pearl grips. They were simply staring ahead whereas all the other passengers were occupied doing something. Branch could not figure out these two hombres, but he knew he had to watch them. Since there were two passenger cars, he walked outside on the steel platform and jumped over the coupling to go check out the other car. That car was mostly families with children and a church group of ladies. There weren't any passengers giving him a furtive look, and so he returned to his car reassured.

Branch read two of the books that covered jungle warfare. As he read them, he started making a list of the traps and contraptions necessary. All these items caused surprise, pain and total demoralization or disability. But most did not kill. The one jungle tool he liked the most was dynamite, because one well-placed stick would get control of a gang or disable several out of the game.

The midnight snack was cookies, donuts, milk and coffee. Afterwards, Branch hit the sack. He included his firearms and both saddlebags in the ample berth made for two. Falling asleep immediately, he slept thru all the refueling stops and even the one hour stop in Walsenburg. At 6AM, the conductor announced that breakfast was being served; and the train would be arriving in La Junta at 9AM.

After morning ablutions and a full filling breakfast, Branch settled back at reading book #3 when his concentration was broken by the loud and harsh words, "LISTEN UP PEOPLE,

THIS IS A ROBBERY." There in front of him was an arrogant piss-ant holding that pearl handle Peacemaker while his two sycophants were holding bags to collect money and jewelry. Person after person, the wallets and reticules were emptied into the burlap bags. One older well-dressed gentlemen appeared in a quandary. When the bag arrived, this businessman refused to open his briefcase and instead he pulled a mini pistol and shot the collecting sycophant in the kneecap.

At that instant, the die was cast. The arrogant piss-ant had his pistol cocked and pointed at the face of the businessman. In slow motion, the businessman closed his eyes knowing that he was about to die. Branch stood up and yelled out, "put that gun down or you're dead." The outlaw smiled and started to turn his pistol towards Branch. The mare's let came out at lightning speed and a single boom was heard that decapitated the outlaw. The third outlaw holding the bag of money literally passed out and collapsed while the one with a blown-out kneecap started throwing up when he saw his partner with a stump pumping blood everywhere.

Shortly, the conductor arrived at a huff, opened the door to the passenger car and walked right in the squirt of the pumping stump, slipped in the blood and fell in the bloody pool. Seeing the stump, the conductor said, "Mister Litchfield, where are you, are you Ok?" "I'm here Samuel, and thanks to this young man I survived my stupidity."

Helpers arrived, the two living outlaws were manacled to seats and the corpse wrapped up in a blanket. The blood was cleaned up and Conductor Samuel came to speak to Branch. "Once we arrive in La Junta, Sheriff McBride will take over the prisoners, you'll have to write a statement and the sheriff will check to see if these three are wanted by the law. For now, please follow me to the private dining car, Mister Litchfield wishes to visit with you." "Who is this man anyways?" "Why he is the owner of this section of railroad from La Junta to Durango."

*

Stepping in the private car, it was clear that the man was still stressed out as he was wiping his face and drinking some fancy whiskey. "Please sit-down young man. My name is Walter Litchfield and you are?" "Branch West—bounty hunter. Why did you risk getting shot for the contents of a briefcase?" "Because, I had just been in Durango to collect our fees from thirty miners and the smelter. I am carrying $100,000 in paper currency which my company could not afford to lose. When the man presented the bag, I forgot that he had two partners, so I decided to shoot him instead of giving my money. Reality set in when the leader put his pistol in my face. I knew my error and that I was going to die, so I closed my eyes to not see the hammer fall. The rest is your doing."

Silence followed for several minutes. Branch broke the moment by saying, "well, you have to admit there was some humor in the tragedy. When the Conductor entered, he got sprayed with blood and then slipped and fell on his butt in a pool of blood. To top it all, when he saw the stump, he called your name thinking maybe the corpse was you, heh?"

Silence again filled the room. This time Walter started laughing. "You are a wise young man, thank you for snapping me out of my misery. Now what do I owe you for my life?" "Not a thing sir, I am a bounty hunter and if these three idiots had horses, I will get them, their guns and their bounty if one was posted." "Well, I owe you and I'll never forget it. One day, we'll again make contact and I will be able to repay your benevolence. For now, Thank You."

*

Arriving at the La Junta train depot, Branch saw an older man standing on the platform. The conductor was first to step off the train as he spotted the man waiting, "Sheriff McBride, how did you know I needed you?" "I didn't, I'm here to pick up someone with the moniker of 'the Mare's Leg Kid.'" "I may be wrong, but I suspect that is Branch West, the man who stopped the train robbery. You have two live outlaws; one needs a new kneecap, one needs a bath, and one headless corps needs to be buried."

Once the outlaws were disposed of, the horses stabled in a livery, the firearms and personal belongings brought to the sheriff's office, they headed off to a diner for dinner.

Waiting for their meal, Sheriff McBride said, "so why are you called the Mare's Leg Kid." "I guess it was Sheriff Watson that coined the title. He must have figured that a kid could only demand respect if he carried a name that implied, I was a shootist with a reputation. I don't like it, but it is the nature of the beast, heh?"

After their meal arrived, they ate their meatloaf/mashed potatoes/peas in silence. Then over several pots of coffee, Sheriff McBride explained why he had requested help. "La Junta has become a haven of undesirables since the railroad came to town. It is an end of road railroad town with a round house and a repair shop. It is also an intersection of many roads and other railroads as well. Consequently, it has become a center of entertainment to include bawdy houses, gambling, dance halls, and saloons. I have managed, with three deputies, to keep the town fairly safe for our residents and workers. The problem is the roads coming to town."

"Really, please explain and how I may help you."

"The saloons and gambling halls are full of card sharks, flimflam artists, drunks, saddle bums, and wanted outlaws. The point is, that most of these deplorables, don't work for a living. Liquor, women and gambling are expensive. In time these footpads realized that robbing pedestrians and local businesses in the streets of their playground, was not the smartest thing to do. So all these losing four flushers need cash and the place to get it is along the five roads coming to town. Yes, highwaymen have become the plague of our community."

"I see where this is going. You want me to pose as a well to do rancher traveling the roads to catch those travelers who try to waylay me."

"Yes sir. I will give you all my current wanted posters, so you'll know who has a bounty. Those without bounties just need to be run out of town.

I'm sure you can convince them, out of fear of bodily harm, to ride faraway and never come back."

"That's a noble goal, but likely these highwaymen are wanted dead or alive. Ok, I accept the job and will start as soon as I gear up for the trail."

*

Picking up vittles and several special contraptions, Branch went to work that same afternoon. He had been on the trail heading northwest out of town when three riders appeared a mile away and heading towards him. Branch stopped Chester, pulled his mare's leg and held it on the saddle pommel. The three riders looked like cowboys. As they approached, the leader started talking. "Howdy, where you headed?" "To Pueblo on business." "Well, we're done cowpunching for the week and headed to town for some fun and drinking. Have a nice day."

As the three riders rode by, they all doffed their hats and smiled. Branch was about to put his mare's leg away when he heard the traveler's horses do some noisy hoof work. Chester spontaneously did an about face, turned 180 degrees, and there I was looking down the barrel of three Colt revolvers.

"Well I'll be darned, it's bad enough being a greenhorn, but when your horse has more living skills than its owner, it's time to smarten up." "Too late for that buster, we want to see what you have in those two saddlebags, and it better be money." "Naw, just junk. My money is in my money belt, and you'll have to shoot me for that."

"Well it's three guns against one, so, if you want to live, you'd better put down that shotgun." "Naw, before your pea brain even thinks of pulling your hammers back, you're going to be plastered with OO Buckshot and be rolling head over heels over your horses' rumps—dead before you hit the ground."

Time stopped, Branch entered that slow-motion trance, saw the outlaws lift their pistol muzzle up, touched the hammer spur, *time to kill or be killed,* and the mare's leg roared BANG-BANG-BANG. All three outlaws were blown off the saddles, as Chester never moved even with the three shotgun blasts next to his ears.

Branch arrived at the sheriff's office an hour later with the three bodies and the three wanted posters. Sheriff McBride listened to the story and said he would apply for the bounty and settle later. Branch headed east to set up a visible camp on the trail. Finding the ideal location with large oak trees to hide behind, Branch set up camp with a large campfire visible for miles. After setting multiple boobytraps on the path from the road to his camp, Branch made his supper with a fresh pot of coffee. After supper, he set himself by the campfire, careful not to look into the fire to maintain his night vision.

A few hours later, he heard some vague rustling of leaves followed by two very clear SNAPS and one ouch, "I stepped on a frigging nail." The two snared ones were groaning and near passing out. "Well boys, that's what you get for walking into someone's camp after dark, and holding your pistols in your hands. Now drop them, or you're dead."

The pistols went flying, but one outlaw yelled out, HELP. At the same time, Chester nickered with a high pitch of surprise. Branch knew he had screwed up again. There was obviously another outlaw about. Branch instantly turned around and fell to his knees, as he fired at a man holding a rifle on him. The OO Buck pellets went high and tore the man's neck apart. He collapsed as if he had been decapitated.

Walking to the man with a nail in his foot, Branch nonchalantly grabbed his boot and yanked the nail out. The outlaw yelled out in pain. "Oh, I forgot to say this might hurt since the nail was jagged. Now get up you weasel and open the traps holding your partners. You animals are lucky I used smooth traps without teeth, cause I've got some bear traps that will cut your boot and your leg off."

Delivering his three outlaws, they were identified as men wanted by the law. Sheriff McBride said, "I'll add these men to the list, check them for money, send for their bounties, sell their horses and firearms. We'll settle later again. Now where you heading next?" "I don't know, any ideas or recommendations?"

"Well it so happens that I do. The merchants are complaining that the influx of hides from the Cheyenne Reservation have drastically reduced, and Pueblo reports a definite increase in available hides. My deputy went to check with the Indian Agent and found out that several Indians, on route to La Junta, had disappeared along with their cargoes."

"Got it, I'll patrol the northern route to Cheyenne country and see what I come up with."

After replenishing his vittles, he started at a slow trot to the northern road. By the end of the day, Branch was about to set up camp when he noticed a wagon stopped some 200 yards ahead. Walking Chester to the wagon, he saw that the wheel had fallen off the axle and an Indian was standing next to the bare axle. "Hello there, looks like you could use some help." "Yes, I could, but not wise for white man seen helping an Indian!" "Well, I won't tell if you don't. Stepping down, Branch introduced himself and presented his hand. The Indian reacted by saying, "my name is PF Silver, and unless you are not 'counting coup,' I would be happy to share the white man's greeting sign."

"Ok, well let's get a long pole to make a fulcrum and jack that axle up. During the process of reattaching the wheel with the retaining ring and cross bolt pin, Branch asked what the PF meant in his name. "When I was born, our chief came to see me. When he stepped out of the teepee, my father (a white man) asked him what I looked like and what would be my name. The chief looked about, saw a silver fox running in the distance and said, 'Pale Face Silver.' Yes, it is clear that I am a half-breed."

Branch then mentioned that they might set up a night camp together in view of the recent robberies and presumed murders. PF agreed, set off to unhitch his horse as Branch unsaddled his. When asked what they were bringing to the supper menu? PF said, I have some sweet pemmican. Branch admitted he had the 'white man' standard of coffee, beans, bacon, and biscuits. PF said, "great, the pemmican will be our dessert with a second pot of coffee. "So, what are you doing on the trail, by your lonesome, with a full load of hides. "My chief, Chief Blue Sky, is sending me to confront the outlaws. You see, I am a pistol gunfighter by self-training and the chief feels I am capable of putting an end to these depredations. Yes, it is strange that for years, the white man suffered from Indian depredations, and now the coin, as you say, has turned. And what are you doing, riding on this dangerous trail?"

"I am an independent bounty hunter sent here by Sheriff McBride to try to capture these hide marauders." "Humm, I am not a superstitious one, but I wonder if there is not a higher power that brought us together this day." "Look down the road, I think that answer will become clear."

Four men were approaching at a full gallop to create the impression of unmatchable power. The group, wearing face bandanas, came to a stop only 20 yards from Branch and PF as the apparent leader said, "leave the hides, guns and horses, and we'll give you one chance to get out alive. You can walk back to town or we'll kill you where you stand."

"Not going to happen, I'm a bounty hunter and I'm arresting you for aggravated assault and attempted robbery." "What is wrong with you, you stupid kid! Can't you see there are four of us against you and 'Kemosabe' here." "Naw, I only need to put two of you down with my sawed-off shotgun, and Mister Silver will put two of your toadies down in the dirt."

"Suit yourselves, go ahead boys, put those two 'idjits' down and let's head to Pueblo with those horses, their guns, that wagon, and those hides."

Branch saw that slow-motion trance begin, with pistols coming out, Branch let go two quick shots and cleared two horse saddles. At the same time PF fired his S&W Frontier Model in 44-40 by fanning it once after his first shot, and both outlaws were on the ground howling in pain as both were holding their shooting arm's shoulder with their left hand. Just as the fight seemed over, PF turned 180 degrees and fired at a bush some 50+ yards away. An outlaw jumped up, dropped his rifle and collapsed in place.

"Dag nab-bit, that's the third time this week that someone tries to shoot me in the back. I'm beginning to think that I'll never learn to protect my back!" "No white man, you need someone to watch your back when dealing with outlaws out to kill you."

After sterilizing the two shoulder wounds, and loading all five outlaws, dead or alive, they made their way back to Sheriff's McBride's office. On the way Branch asked PF what his background was. "I was raised along the Indian tradition but my father, the Indian agent and Chief Blue Sky insisted I get your white man schooling to 10th grade. Along the same time I trained myself to draw and shoot my S&W. They now want me to get some higher education, but I refused. My responsibility to my tribe and family is to trap furs for the income to help feed my tribe in the reservation."

"Why does the name Chief Blue Sky ring a bell?" "Because he was an acquaintance of Wayne Swanson, the bounty hunter/US Marshal." "Oh yes, the book by Swanson."

After some traveling and using time to think, Branch finally said. "have you ever considered becoming a bounty hunter instead of a trapper?"

"I guess I never thought of killing white men for money." "It's not white men, it's evil outlaws that are wanted dead or alive for abhorrent crimes against humanity—usually kidnapping, robbery or murder."

"How much does it pay; it's going to be hard to beat the $125 value of my load of furs gathered over three months." "Are you for real, the two men with shoulder injuries and the one you killed are wanted men and all three will pay you $1,500." "WHAT, that's insane." "It is what it is and these prices were set by reputable people, lawmen, and are upheld by the courts. But, the profession is very dangerous, since you are dealing with the worse humans that want to kill you."

"Humm, are you looking for an employee to watch your back?"

"No, I'm looking for a partner to share the responsibility and the spoils at 50/50.

"Not interested, but I'll take the job at 60/40 since the boss always makes the most money."

"DEAL." The contract was sealed with the white man's word—a handshake.

*

That same day, Sheriff McBride took in the two injured outlaws and arranged for the local Doc to see them. Then he said, "That's the fourth group you have brought in—three men from the train robbery, three from being waylaid, four from attacking your camp, and now these five from the attempted robbery of furs. If you stay over a couple days, I will have sold all the horses, firearms and have collected the Western Union vouchers to cover the bounties." "Ok, we certainly can enjoy a few days of city living, hot meals and a real bed. See you in two days."

The Duo registered at the La Junta General and took two rooms. In the morning, they enjoyed a grand breakfast of steak and eggs with two pots of coffee. PF mentioned, "As a half breed working with a white man, I think I should look as Americanized as possible. So I need cowboy boots and a cowboy hat, blue jeans, a nice bib shirt, and a leather vest. Then I need a haircut and a bath." "Fine, let's go shopping before we hit the tonsorial shop."

It was noon before the Duo looked like new in their new duds and a haircut. Branch also had a shave. PF asked, "what do I look like, an Indian, a half breed or a white man?" "Well you still have the high cheek bones, a whiskerless face, and a slight copper tone skin of a Cheyenne, but the blue eyes and your modern fancy clothing makes you look like a city dude. I guess you really look like a half breed, but sticking with me, you'll get more and more Americanized over time. If there is any question, we'll get you some stogies and chewing tobacco."

After a chicken pie dinner, while planning their afternoon, it came to Branch that PF did not have a riding horse. "Let's visit the liveries and find you a non-descriptive horse that is not an eye sore. After the third livery, a 17-hand chestnut Quarter Horse gelding was found. It was similar to Branch's Chester except for the long white blade on his forehead with black points. Chester was a pure chestnut without points of any kind. PF chose one of four saddles and tack and left with two saddlebags, and a rifle scabbard for $115.

The Duo then finished the day by filling the saddlebags with personal items for the trail. Before supper, they visited a gun shop to buy PF a rifle. PF wanted a rifle good to 250 yards with the velocity to put an outlaw down at that range. The gunsmith commented, "Winchester is working on such a rifle with the new smokeless powder and copper jacketed bullets in 30-30 caliber. For now, the best we have is the Win 73 in 44-40 or to the big gun Win 76 in 45-70." "Branch added, "Since I have the big gun in 45-70, I suggest you take a Win 73 in the same caliber as our pistols until this new rifle becomes available." Leaving with a new Win 73 and a case of 44-40 ammo, the Duo was planning to do some practice shooting tomorrow morning.

After a nice supper of prime rib au jus, mashed potatoes and fresh peas, the Duo went looking for a cold beer. Entering the Super Mug

Saloon, the bartender gave the Duo a quick look and asked, "what can I get you gents? PF said, "some cold beers, and we'll sit on the porch if that is what you prefer." "Nonsense, half-breeds are welcomed in my bar, and that's all I'll say on the subject. Take a table and I'll bring you your beers."

Drinking their beer, Branch said, "I didn't expect any less from the barkeep. What I worry about are some drunks short of a load that want to throw us out. Just finishing his last words, a cowboy tapped PF on the shoulder, "you're an Indian and we don't allow Indians in this bar." The barkeep came over and said, "Stinky, this is the famous bounty hunter called The Mare's Leg Kid and this is his new partner, Mister Silver. These two men have now brought in 18 outlaws, dead or alive." "I don't care, Indians are not allowed in my bar." "This is not your bar you idjit. It's my bar and you're out of here." Stinky's feet never touched the floor and he was catapulted thru the bat wing doors.

After the incident, PF came out with a meaningful thought. "Never humiliate a man, rich or poor, without expecting retribution in the form of a bullet."

"Well said, now this is the right time to tell you about some basic rules I try to follow. Going over Sheriff Watson words of wisdom, he emphasized the rule "it's time to kill or be killed." Branch added, "shooting an outlaw in his shooting arm or shoulder may work 99% of the time, but when you miss, you'll be dead. You have to remain alive and not wounded to do this profession."

The next day was settling with Sheriff McBride. The sheriff had his figures ready and started, I sold 12 horses with saddle and tack for $90X12=$1080. I sold 14 pistols for $350 and 14 rifles for $490. The bounties of 15 outlaws came to four leaders and eleven gang members. The leaders were worth $1,000 each and the gang members for $500 each. The grand total comes to $11,420"

On the spot, Branch gave the sheriff $500 for organizational assistance, $50 for the undertaker, $50 for feeding outlaws in jail. On their way to the Community Bank, Branch hands

PF $1,500 as his share, and was then left with $9,320. After bank accounts were established, Branch left with $320 and PF left with $1,050 in cash.

The next day, PF went to the Cheyenne reservation to say his goodbyes. He left $1,000 with Chief Blue Sky and explained that he was entering a new profession that would help support the tribe. When the money was gone, the Chief was told to make contact with Sheriff McBride for more money.

When he returned to the hotel, he went to Branch's room and simply said, "Ok Boss, I'm at your service. Let's go to work, heh?"

***

CHAPTER 3

The Early Capers

Meeting with Sheriff McBride, the Duo realized that an exodus of undesirables had occurred in town since the last batch of dead or crippled friends had been deposited either at the undertakers or in jail awaiting trial and likely hanging. Sheriff McBride started, "If I was you, I'd go where the outlaws are and where the big money is, and that's not here. You did a fine job here, but now I would head north from Pueblo to Denver. If you want to stop in Pueblo, I'll send word to Sheriff McBain of your arrival and I'll include my recommendation."

Branch looked at PF for his opinion and was surprised at his answer, "it's 70 miles to Pueblo and we'll have to do it on horses since the railroad doesn't connect La Junta and Pueblo. I suspect we'll meet up with highwaymen on the two-day ride, and capturing them would be a great introduction with Sheriff McBain."

"Sounds like a plan. Let's load up with supplies and be on our way." While they saddled their horses, Branch said, "so what are you naming your horse. "My people don't name our horses, but working as a white man I will call him 'Hoss.'"

Riding at a slow trot PF noticed a large dust cloud on their backtrail and shortly afterwards recognized the local stagecoach. The Duo stepped off the road and let the coach pass by. The jeju and shotgun guard waved as the team was at a full trot with a coach full of passengers. Within five minutes several rifle and pistol gun shots were heard. PF said, "there were no shotgun blasts, those boys are in trouble." At a full gallop, the Duo arrived and found the jeju bandaging the guard's arm. Branch yelled, "what happened?" "Outlaws blocked the road with a tree and wounded Charlie. They stole the strong box, which had bank transfer money, and the passengers' wallets. They just took off. I'm sure they were the notorious Musgrove gang." "We're going after them if you can manage removing that tree." "Will do, but be careful these are known killers."

"Let's push hard while they're on the road, if they get off or we spot them ahead, then we'll slow down." With the prairie lands, the gang was quickly spotted some two miles ahead. To avoid creating a dust cloud the Duo slowed to a fast walk. An hour later, PF spotted the area where they veered off and went cross-country. Moving slowly PF stopped and said, "I can smell wood smoke, and it's a cabin because I smell stovepipe creosote." "Hell, I can't even smell smoke and you can smell creosote? Really," BANG. "Yep, that's them, they just shot the lock and opened the strong box. We got them now. Let's hobble our horses, put our moccasins and head out with a bear trap and a half stick of dynamite." "Sounds like fun to me."

The cabin was a shack that was falling down. The outlaws were heard dividing the money as

PF climbed up to the roof next to the stove pipe. The outlaw leader must have heard PF and sent one of his toadies to see what the noise was. Stepping thru the door's threshold a loud snap was heard followed by a scream that startled Branch. The snap was the sign for PF to drop the half stick down the stovepipe. The leader opened the door to see his man on the floor with his leg nearly cut off. At that instant the dynamite went off, blew the stove apart, propelled the leader over the porch, the windows blew out and two walls collapsed. The other two outlaws came out full of soot, barely able to walk and fell to the ground. Leaving their buddy still stuck in the bear trap.

The four outlaws were shackled with manacles. The bear trap victim was bandaged, and the outlaws' pockets emptied. A total of $1142 was found in pocket cash. PF went in the shack and found a saddlebag. Inside was $10,000 in currency identified by a 1st National Bank band, plus six wallets with plenty of money.

The Duo loaded their prisoners, collected their sooty guns, and headed back to La Junta.

When they arrived, everyone was surprised since no one knew the stage had been robbed and the money stolen. Sheriff McBride checked out the outlaws and said that they were wanted outlaws with a sizeable bounty. The bank president asked if the money was recovered. Branch responded, "well that depends if there was a reward." "There was none posted since I didn't know it was stolen." "Well now you know, so is there a reward or not?" "A usual reward is 10% and the bank will honor that." "Ok, here is your money, a bit sooty and smelly, but I want clean smelling cold cash, thank you."

The sheriff comes out of his office saying that the outlaws had a total of $2,500 in bounty." "Good, sell the horses and firearms and keep $300 for yourself. Put the value of horses, guns, the bounty and the bank reward balance in our bank accounts split 50/50. Pf objected and said, "didn't I say 60/40?" "You did, but I said 50/50, and I'm the boss, heh? Also, see to it that the wallets are returned to their rightful owners."

*

Heading to Pueblo and getting close to sunset, the Duo had not met a single traveler as they approached a small town called Fowler. Branch had an idea, "let's stop in town, get a beer and talk to the bartender. We'll tell him we're on route to Pueblo for business purposes, and talk loud enough for patrons to hear. We'll leave our guns in the saddlebags and we'll appear as good candidates for a robbery. Then we'll take off and make camp close to the road—the good trusting souls we are, heh?" "Huum, isn't that called entrapment?" "Yes, but if we only entrap wanted outlaws, we're doing society a favor, heh?"

Their mission completed; the Duo set up camp some five miles away. Starting a good fire as a beacon, the Duo prepared their meal of beef stew and canned potatoes. After several coffees, the Duo decided to prepare for visitors with nefarious intent. They built up the fire, stuffed their bedrolls with grass, and laid out two bear traps behind the camp to catch rear entry back shooters. The third bear trap was set on the trail from the road. They then moved out of the campsite area. Branch hid behind a large oak tree for protection while watching the trail from the road. PF was watching the back of the camp while hidden up a large pine tree.

A few hours later, the clip-pity-clop of horses' hooves was heard. Eventually, in the clear moonlit night, five horsemen arrived. One was dispatched, on foot, to our left flank. The other four waited for their buddy to get into place as they secured their horses away from the trail to the camp. After a waiting period, the four outlaws started creeping toward the campfire. Fifteen yards from the bedrolls, Branch heard that pleasing sound-SNAP.

Amidst loud screams, the other three miscreants fired their pistols repeatedly at the two stuffed bedrolls. Branch was twenty yards away, sneaked to the side of his tree and let go BOOM,BOOM,BOOM. The spray of #3 Buck with its twenty .25-inch pellets was a shower of 'angry hornets' causing death and misery. All three shooting outlaws were down as Branch reloaded his lever shotgun and walked up to the outlaws. One was dead with several pellet hits to the head, while the other two shooters had multiple non-lethal hits. "Well, don't you birdbrains look smart. I suspect we'll find some paper on you boys, and your future is guarded. SNAP. Oh gosh, that was your buddy, I don't think he's in any mood to back shoot us, heh?" Next, in the back of the camp, PF yelled, "throw your pistol and rifle away from you. If you don't, then I'm going to leave you in the trap as bait for the wolves, hah!"

After releasing the two snared victims, PF cleansed, sterilized and bandaged the wounds. Each outlaw was manacled to an individual tree, their horses hobbled onto good grass and the Duo finally got a good night sleep in well-ventilated bedrolls. In the morning, PF started breakfast as Branch emptied the outlaws' pockets and saddlebags. He collected $412, which he gave half to PF, and a bank bag containing $10,500.

The ride to Pueblo was an audible cacophony of moans and groans from painful legs or buckshot in a multitude of places. The 25-mile ride was quickly traveled on the good road to Pueblo. Once in town, they rode straight to the sheriff's office. Sheriff McBain came outside to see who had arrived as PF spoke, "my name is PF Silver, and this is my boss, Branch West, aka The Mare's Leg Kid. We were attacked last night, and we are bringing you the Wilson Gang. Four need a doctor, one needs an undertaker, and we need a shave, a bath, and a hot meal" "I know who you are from Sheriff McBride's telegram. How do you know this is the Wilson Gang that robbed and killed a customer three weeks ago, and left with over $10,000?" "Because I saw the wanted posters while in La Junta, and Branch adds, "plus we have the bank bag, and the exact amount is $10,500— of which we expect a reward of 10% or more." "Fair enough, get cleaned up, I'll process the horses, firearms, apply for their bounty, and get your bank recovery reward. See me in two days for breakfast at Wilma's Place."

*

That evening they took two rooms in the Pueblo Queen Hotel, got a shave and a bath, changed their clothes and had a great supper at Wilma's Place. After a full night's sleep and a complete breakfast in the hotel's restaurant. The Duo then went for a walk. The town was more like a small city. Specialized mercantiles and evidence of railroad commerce was the norm. Walking into a general store, they bought a clothing replacement and some ammo. While waiting to pay for their goods, Branch heard a few guys discuss a horse ranch that was producing riding mounts and racehorses.

With nothing to do but wait for the sheriff, after dinner, the Duo decided to visit that horse ranch. The hostler helped saddle their horses and gave them directions to the Double A ranch. The short three-mile ride to the horse ranch ended when a high arched gate, marked with the AA logo, was seen at the entrance to the access road. Arriving at the main house, an elderly gentleman was rocking on the porch. "What brings you young fellas to my ranch. We sell horses, are you interested in riding mounts, harness horses, show horses or racehorses? The Duo looked at each other and each hoped the other would answer. Branch unconsciously said, "racehorses."

"Well, come along then, and my name is Anson Aiken. We sell the American Quarter Horse who is well known to run a quarter mile in 20-22 seconds. Here is a paddock of thirty 12-18-month old fillies and colts. Walk among them and see if there is one you particularly like. Branch walked thru the herd and realized he had no idea what he was looking for. As he walked away, PF was intently checking each horse and then taking a staring position for three horses followed by a slow blink of the eyes.

Branch finally said, "what did you just do that was special for three horses?" "I made a photographic image in my brain of those horses, the same process when I saw the Wilson Gang's wanted posters. Incidentally, the reward on those five is $3,500."

"So what is so special about those horses?" "Notice how alert and bright they appear among people. They walk lively without moping along. Their hooves are not pigeon toed or splayed. The front shoulders and hind end are very muscular. The tail is up and strong; and their legs are not 'cow-hocked' with the rear legs too close at the hooves—known to ruin hips. They have nice balance and a high head, plus they are friendly"

"So, you're saying that these are likely to be good runners?" "No boss, I'm saying they will be winning racehorses and good breeding stock to raise."

"Well boys, anyone strike your fancy?" PF answered, "colt #3 and fillies #17 & 27." "Wow, you know horses, those are certainly my choices." Branch took over. "How much to buy those three horses?"

"Well, let me explain the marketing and sale of racehorses. These 18-month old horses will now slowly start training. Today, I take a deposit of $2,000 each and in 24 months or sooner, if they can run a quarter mile in 20-22 seconds, then you pay me another $1,000 and walk away with the horse. If anyone fails the 20-22 second test, I refund your money, or you can take the horse without any more payment. If you cancel before six months, you get all your money back. If you cancel after six months you get 50% of your investment back"

Branch never hesitated, as he handed Mister Aiken a bank draft for $6,000. The rancher looked at the draft and said, "looks like we need to sign some contracts to make the deal legal." "Ok, and I'll be back in 18 months from today or sooner."

On their way back to town, PF smiled as he thought about the deal Branch had made. It was not till after supper that PF asked, "why did you make that deal today, wasn't that possibly premature?" "No, my plans include bounty hunting until I enter the Lawman School this fall, and then apply for a position on the US Marshal Service. Living by the gun will eventually come to an end when my debt to a higher power is paid. Then, I will find a piece of land or buy an existing ranch and raise horses for a living. So, it was not premature, but it actually was part of my destiny."

*

The next morning, Sheriff McBain was waiting for the Duo at Wilma's Place. He had a cup of coffee in his hands as he rocked away on the porch. "It's about time you got your butts up, I'm getting hungry!"

"Great, how about steak, eggs and home-fries with coffee, on us?" "Thought you'd never ask!" After putting their order in, the sheriff started settling finances. "Five pistols and rifles=$300. Five horses with saddle and tack= $450. Bounty rewards= $3,500. Bank reward=$1,500." "Great, here is $500 for your help and $75 for the doctor. The remainder will go in our new bank accounts in the Wells Fargo Bank of Pueblo."

Once their meals arrived, more discussion was put off. Afterwards, Sheriff McBain started, "so, where are you heading next?" "Well my partner here has a photographic memory. So, after he looks at your wanted posters, I guess we'll start visiting your saloons and hopefully find some owlhoots to arrest." "Well after the sweep, come and see me as I have an idea for your next caper."

It took two hours to review the wanted posters as PF took at least 50 shots for his brain banks. Come sunset, the Duo set out to visit the saloons.

The first saloon on the strip was the Sunset Haven with working gals, meals, and rooms to rent. The Duo walked in and stepped to the bar. With a beer in their hands, PF scouted the patrons by looking in the full mirror behind the bartender. In no time he said, "we're in luck, the Boyd Gang of four outlaws is sitting on our far right against the wall. Remember once we turn around, they will be on our far left. Boyd himself is wearing a large white hat with a tall crown. They are wanted for kidnapping, murder, and torture. The bounty is $4,000 which means they are very dangerous killers. Better plan on a gunfight."

Meanwhile, the bartender was listening and heard Branch say, "I'll pretend to walk to the back door for the privy but will do a quick stop at their table. You move to the right to flank them and cover my back." PF looks at the bartender and says, "barkeep, unload that shotgun under the bar or you'll likely get shot during the gunfight."

When the bar patrons saw what the bartender was doing, they started scattering or stepping outside. Branch was walking when he drew his Mare's Leg and yelled, "this is the end of the line Boyd, stand up all four of you and put your hands up." "That's not gonna happen you punk kid, so make your play or get out of my face." "I've made my play, it's now your turn puke face." Boyd was red face and fuming. His three sycophants turned to face Branch, and suddenly PF fired and an outlaw, holding his pistol pointing right at Branch, collapsed to the floor as he discharged his pistol in the floor sawdust.

"Ah hah, so you were going to win this gunfight by ambushing me, heh? Well my partner evened the odds, now it's me against you four. Put your hands up or DRAW." As if the starting gun started the race, all four outlaws went for their pistols as everyone heard KABOOM-BOOM-BOOM-BOOM. The room was filled with the acrid smoke, but Branch stepped up to make sure the outlaws were dead. Once the smoke cleared the outlaws were dragged outside to wait for the undertaker as Sheriff McBain arrived.

After checking out the dead men's faces, the sheriff said, "I see you started cleaning the city of its resident trash. That's the Boyd Gang, but why are there five members? PF said, "must be they added a recent member who was hidden in the crowd as their backup, but was not known to the law." Branch was looking at that fifth man and said, "well, this time you shot for the head instead of the shoulder, you must be learning!" "No, I didn't have a choice since his hammer was pulled back, I needed to get a kill shot, so I shot him in the ear. The result was a dramatic body 'fold up' with the pistol barrel turning to the floor before discharging. I won't forget this technique, heh?"

Sheriff McBain took care of removing the bodies, collecting the firearms and pocket cash. He used the pocket cash to pay for the room/meal/bar tab, the blood cleanup and repairing the holes in the wall. Meanwhile the Duo decided to continue their sweep.

The next three saloons were clean of wanted outlaws. The fourth one was another nest of two outlaw gangs. PF pointed out the Mathews

Gang of three murdering bank robbers and the Freeman Gang of five train robbers who had derailed a train and killed seven passengers. Branch pointed out that that the two gangs were separated by a table of locals. Finally, PF said, "maybe we should skip this one, heh." "Nah, this is a hay-day and we'll work it safely to our benefit. This is what I propose: We'll nonchalantly walk to the Mathews Gang and buffalo all three till they are knocked out. Then I'll yell to that table of locals to get out to clear the path to the five Freeman outlaws. I'll put three down on the left and you put the two on the right—down means dead, right?" "Right."

Before finishing their beer, the bartender did the deed of unloading the bar shotgun. Afterwards, the Duo walked to the Mathews' table as Branch smacked two on the head with his shotgun while PF did the third one. Branch then yelled at the table of locals; you boys get out—NOW. There was no hesitation as the path was cleared to Freeman's table. "Freeman, you and your bunch of nitwits are under arrest for train derailment, robbery and deaths resulting.

Now get up and put your hands up." PF then yells, "the rest of you get out of here—NOW."

Freeman finally spoke, "well this is a sudden revolting development. Now there are five of us and two of you. Isn't that nice. Now you may get some of us, but we'll get all of you. If you smart alecks have any brains you'll walk out now—this is your only chance."

"Not gonna happen, you are worth too much dead or alive. So make your play, we're ready. As if on cue, hands went for their gun grip as the saloon was filled with BOOM-BOOM-BANG-BOOM-BANG. The outside patrons came rushing to the batwing doors to see the results, as the smoke filled the entire saloon and the Duo nonchalantly walked outside to reload their guns.

Sheriff McBain again showed up and was informed that the Mathews Gang was alive and unconscious, and the Freeman Gang was ready for the undertaker. The sheriff walked in, put manacles on the Mathews Gang, and checked out the five dead outlaws. As he came back outside, he said, "that's a lot of dead outlaws and enough live ones to fill my cells. I hope that does it for tonight since this old man has to get some sleep." "Yeah, we agree. If you pay the bartender for damages and the undertaker for services, we'll help you tomorrow to collect the cash, sell the horses and guns, and workout the bounties on record." "Fair enough, see you at Bernie's Diner for breakfast."

*

The Duo was early at the diner but Sheriff McBain was nowhere in sight. Sitting on the boardwalk porch, with coffee, they waited. At 9AM the sheriff dragged himself to the diner. "Wow, what a night. The three hostlers were up all-night getting customer horses ready for riding. It seemed that every unknown visitor was leaving town after your last double arrest. Guess they suspected they would be next, heh?" "So why did that affect you?" "Because, they were trying to leave without paying their stable bills. My presence on the street changed that real quick, but I didn't get to bed till 3AM." "Well, let's get some breakfast and we'll discuss this recent development."

The late breakfast menu was an extra-large serving of the daily special—scrambled eggs, strip bacon, home-fries and endless coffee. Their meal came quickly, and the business meeting was held up while they ate. "Today, I'm going to send the telegrams requesting payment for the Boyd, Mathews, and Freeman gangs. Payment by telegraph voucher should arrive by late afternoon." "If you do that, we'll visit the gun shops and liveries to sell the firearms and horses. Then we'll deposit the funds and wait by midafternoon at the telegraph office for you."

"Now, let's talk about your next caper. I think the gravy is gone out of this town, especially with the exodus last night. I hate to see you go, but a good friend of mine, Sheriff Jim Watkins, in Colorado Springs needs help. It appears that a Mega gang has formed with three leaders—Wheeler, Jenkins, and Davidson. Reports of at least 17 outlaws marauding the plains east of Colorado Springs. It appears they attack ranches with three gang members, while five members keep the bunkhouse cowboys under siege. They rape the owner's wife forcing him to open the safe where cash is kept to meet payroll. If the rape doesn't work, then they torture the ladies. These are altruistic animals, and they need to be stopped anyway you can do it."

"Are these outlaws wanted men or is there a reward for their capture?" "Both, there is a $10,000 reward plus I suspect that several have bounties on their heads. The drawback, is that they hide in camps, avoid towns and are on the move every day from ranch to ranch." "I won't deny that this situation demands careful planning, but we can do it. Assuming we finish our business today, we'll be on the train to cover the 45 miles to Colorado Springs and meet with Sheriff Watkins." "Great, the train leaves at 7AM and I'll wire Jim of your arrival in the morning."

The Duo had some difficulty selling 13 horses. The hostler, holding the remuda in his pasture, bought four with complete saddle and tack for $85 each. Competitors were invited to a modified auction and the remaining nine fully dressed horses sold for $90 each because of competitive bidding. Selling 13 pistols and 13 rifles was even more of a challenge. The only gun shop wanted all of them, but could only afford 5 of each for $300. The remaining 16 firearms were sold piecemeal to the many mercantiles in town, but at a slight discount. Normally a pistol and rifle sell for $55 max. The Duo averaged $45 a pair and were satisfied.

Using the two accounts in the Wells Fargo Bank of Pueblo, they deposited $900 in their separate accounts and kept $50 in pocket cash. After a late dinner, the Duo parked themselves in front of the telegraph office. When Sheriff McBain arrived he said, "you boys 'done good' today. The total bounty rewards on those three gangs comes to $10,500 and the vouchers are inside the telegraph office." "Great, here is $500 for your trouble, and we'd appreciate a good word sent to Sheriff Watkins." "Already done. Plan on witling down that gang before you face them."

Before taking the train to Colorado Springs, the Duo visited several stores to buy a multitude of different items that could be used in jungle warfare. PF was the most creative in choosing parts used in building his unique contraptions. Realizing they would be on the trail for this next caper, they decided to purchase a pack horse with a pack saddle and two paniers. Then they added a tarp to make a cover for the horses, two two-man tent in case of rain, extensive hardware for jungle warfare, extra manacles, extra ammo, and extra bedrolls for comfort.

Buying their tickets, their cost was based on short distance rates—90 cents per horse (2 cents per mile) with hay and water, and $1.80 per man (4 cents per mile) with unlimited coffee. With everything loaded, they traveled the 45 miles to Colorado City in an hour and a half compared to an all-day trail ride.

***

CHAPTER 4

The Later Capers

Traveling to the clacking of the steel wheels on the rail connections, and the railcar swaying put Branch to sleep. PF was reading an outline of a course on jungle warfare offered at the Lawman's School in Denver. Unbeknown to PF, Branch had read the same outline months ago along with several books by Swanson, Harnel, Adams and McWain. These were bounty hunters who mastered the new method of subduing and achieving control of an outlaw or a full gang of them.

When they arrived at the platform, PF put his textbook away. Disembarking, Sheriff Watkins was waiting for them. "It was easy recognizing the man wearing a Mare's Leg and standing next to a half native American. PF was stunned and said, "thank you, that's the first time I'm called a half native American instead of a half-breed. That was a nice touch, sir." "You're welcome, now let's have a snack of homemade donuts and coffee at Georgiana's Diner."

After the usual pleasantries, Sheriff Watkins started, "as you know, this marauding mega gang has hit four ranches east of here. I visited all four and got the same story. Eight outlaws show up after the cowboys are off on the range, leaving the owner and his wife alone with the bunkhouse cook and barn wrangler. The rest you know; and two of the wives were raped as well as two of the men were tortured with broken arms. The total money stolen from these four ranchers totaled $17,000. Now my deputy continued east to Ellicott to warn the remaining three ranches to be ready. He even rode east of Ellicott to warn the next three ranches. I have notified the telegraph operator in Ellicott, Yoder and Rush. Any attacks will be reported to me. That covers the 40 miles east of here.

Ranches east of Rush, some 50 miles, are the responsibility of the Aroya sheriff. But keep in mind that the Kansas Pacific railroad comes to Aroya and leads to all points east into Kansas."

Branch asked, "where do the ranchers do their banking?" "In Ellicott or Aroya." "Any doctors in these towns?" "Only in Ellicott and Aroya. "Does Yoder and Rush have any services?" "Yes, a mercantile, a hardware store, a livery/smithy, a saloon at a minimum, and a population of less than 200—just enough to maintain the ranches. Ellicott is a full-service town with a population of 1200 but no lawman."

"Ok, well we'll load up with supplies and be off. We'll do our best to stop this army of outlaws."

"Before you leave, let me deputize you. You'll need that badge because everyone is a bit short fused with strangers. I'll telegraph every community and inform them of your status, and let them know you are the Mare's Leg Kid. If there's any question of your identity, just show them that crazy looking lever action shotgun.

Remember, you'll have to whittle this army down any way you can—17 to 2 is suicide."

*

Once on the trail, PF asked Branch, "how are you working out the plans for this caper, I sure don't like the odds." "Our horses are fresh, so let's push them. We'll skip the four ranches that were robbed and head for the fifth one. We'll go from there, heh."

Arriving at the access road to the fifth ranch, the Duo saw a man sitting on the porch with a shotgun on his lap. He stood up and fired a round. In response, the wife stepped outside with a shotgun in hand, as well as the cook and wrangler came running with shotguns in hand. Branch responded by pulling out a white kerchief for this purpose. The Duo approached under the protection of the white flag.

Riding to the ranch house, the owner said, "I see the badges, let me see your side arms." Branch stood on his stirrups and twisted sideways to expose his Mare's Leg. "That's good enough for me, welcome. How would you like some coffee?"

"No thanks, we're in a hurry. Were you attacked lately?" "Yes, an hour ago. We gave them the same reception we gave you and all eight riders turned around at 100 yards. Guess they didn't like the odds against four double barrel shotguns." "Thanks, how far to your next neighbor?" "Three miles, but they'll be presenting the same reception."

Arriving at the next ranch, they approached with the same white flag after the warning shot. The owner gave the same scenario except he mentioned that the gang did not take the road east, but instead headed north cross-country. The Duo quickly found their tracks and PF led the way.

Meanwhile at the outlaw camp, Wheeler was leading a discussion of today's events. "The ranchers have been warned and are waiting for us. Seems to me we'll find the same thing east of Ellicott. So it is time to change our target or to move on to Kansas. What do you two bosses think?" Jenkins said, "I hate to see ranchers waiting for us. It's a losing proposition. I say we head to Aroya and take the train to Kansas. Davidson then added his two cents, "seems to me that 17 men should be able to take the bank in Ellicott and Aroya before hightailing out to Kansas. Wheeler then asked for a vote and robbing the bank in Elliott was unanimous.

After following the tracks for two hours, PF smelled camp-smoke. The Duo decided to start rattling their cages. Branch set up behind a large rock and set his scoped Win 76 to 400 yards. There was a slight breeze from right to left so he spotted two outlaws standing next to each other. The crosshairs went to the man on the right. As he pulled the trigger, he saw the man on the left get blown over. The result was total pall-mall and bedlam. PF smiled and added, "wow, that camp looks like a hornet's nest that just got wacked with a stick, heh?"

"Oh, oh. We've got a problem. They've got a Sharps rifle and a man is setting up on cross sticks. Bet you he doesn't compensate for the breeze and will end up shooting to my left." Kaboom, and the rock to Branch's left exploded. Branch waited long enough to see the outlaw reloading. As he fired, a metallic spark was seen as the bullet hit the Sharp's hammer and then took off the outlaw's head. PF whispered, "two down, 15 to go. Take another one out and we're 'out a here,' yes sir-ree!"

Branch aimed at an outlaw sitting on his horse and preparing to come and flank them. As he fired, the horses all spooked when the rider was blown off his horse. "Let's get out of here, they'll be coming to flank us. We'll be back tonight to set some booby traps."

Meanwhile, in camp, Wheeler yells out, "you two flank them to the right and you two flank them to the left. If they're gone chase after them for a while to find out what direction they took. The rest of you, close up camp and get ready to ride by the time the boys are back. You four, go after the spooked horses." When the flankers came back, they reported that the shooters were heading north of camp. Wheeler said, "so they are going to spend the night coming full circle behind us to pick us off come sunup. Well, leave the dead men with their horses. I suspect they are bounty hunters who will want to bring the bodies in for the bounty. That will slow them down, and we'll hit the bank before they get to town."

The Duo spent all night making their way to 400 yards north of the outlaw camp. Upon arriving, PF asked Branch if he was going to pick some more off come daylight. "Well, this is war and it's their army against ours. This is not a game with gentlemen rules. It's a matter of killing them or be killed, and who will win the battle. Well, this is not our day to die, so we'll do what we have to do."

PF kept watching the outlaw's campfire and finally said, "something is wrong, it's too cold to have such a small campfire. I'll sneak closer on moccasins and see what is going on. If I fire one shot, bring the horses and walk up to their camp."

When PF got there, he fired his pistol and waited. "Guess you're right. They must have bugged out after our shooting exercise. They left the three dead and their horses because they knew we needed to bring in the bodies if we wanted to get their bounty. So, the gangs must now be camped outside of Ellicott and waiting for the bank to open." PF had a suggestion, "let's carefully make our way south and east of town. We'll set up within 40 yards of the easterly main road, and when they are galloping by to make their escape, we'll let them have some lead and thin out the army again." "Sounds like a plan."

By daybreak, they had hidden the six horses and were standing behind trees by the roadside. PF decided to use a coachgun shotgun which he had purchased as a jungle warfare contraption. He figured that broadside shooting on outlaws at a full gallop was best done with a OO Buckshot loaded scattergun.

Meanwhile, Wheeler and Davidson showed up with the 14-man army. The outlaws placed three men on the western part of Main Street while three men guarded the eastern entry. The remainder of the gang would swamp the bank which was known to be protected by private armed guards. Before entry, Davidson yelled, "shoot the guards and anyone in the way!" The result was a blood bath of four dead, the two guards and a customer and clerk as collateral damage. The wounded president of the bank was coerced to open the vault. The gang then made their escape heading east to get to the train out of state. The three money bags were distributed between three riders as the gang left at a full gallop while shooting up the town.

The Duo waited patiently. Branch was to shoot at the lead riders and PF would shoot at the middle riders. If everything went to plan, they hoped to put down at least 5 dead and several escaping wounded with non-lethal pellets. Out of nowhere the thundering noise of dozens of hooves sounded like the gates of hell had opened up. As the gang arrived, it was a matter of shooting at the masses above the horses' backs; and swinging forward with the pack at high speeds.

By the time the smoke bloom cleared, the remainder of the gang had escaped but several outlaws were leaning in the saddle because of catching some OO Buckshot. On the ground were five dead outlaws and a fatally wounded horse that was immediately shot. The outlaws' pockets and saddlebags were searched and a total of $21,702 was found. The Duo pocketed the $702 and kept the balance as bank property. They then loaded the dead outlaws and rode to town with their eight outlaws and seven outlaw horses.

Arriving in town, there was a crowd gathered in front of the bank. President Thompson greeted the Duo and gave them the bad news of four deaths and $30,000 in currency that had been received to maintain and replenish the payroll fund for all the ranchers within 50 miles. PF then asked, "is there any reward for returning the money?" President Thompson answered, "of course, the usual 10%." "You're kind of cheap, would any man here go after this gang for 10%?" SILENCE "Well then, let's say 20% or we'll keep the heist when we retrieve it, heh?" "OK, 20% it is." Then in that case, here is $21,000 and you owe us $4,200. We'll be back with the other $9,000. And if you want it all, then you'd better come back with a decent compensation package for the family of those dead victims." As the Duo was leaving, Branch asked that a telegram be sent to Sheriff Watkins to send his deputy with wanted posters to ID the dead outlaws. "We'll pay for the undertaker on our return."

The Duo took off and were about to stop at the shootout site to pick up their pack horse when they saw the animal waiting by the road. PF whistled and yelled, "come on Buddy, follow us. We ain't holding your lead rope. Follow or stay here alone." Buddy got right on Hoss's tail as Branch asked, "now how did you know he would follow." "It's simple, have you seen him alone while feeding in the fields, he's always very close to our horses. I'm beginning to think that he's one of those special geldings that likes more than company, heh?" "Really! What's next?"

They traveled till dusk and then set up camp. Feeling that the gang was at least 10 miles still ahead, the Duo set up a full camp with a heating and cooking campfire. The horses cropped grass all night and by early daybreak the Duo was off after a breakfast of hot coffee, beans and leftover hoe cakes.

They traveled all day when suddenly PF lost the tracks. PF went back and spotted where the gang had veered south to circle the town of Aroya. Branch added, "it's too late to enter town tonight, they'll be setting up camp and we'll torment them all night with our doo-dads, heh?"

By midnight, the Duo had sneaked up to within 50 yards of the outlaw camp. Branch had already decided to deliver a decisive blow to the gang and get control of every outlaw right from the start. To accomplish this, the Duo sneaked up to the camp and attached three full sticks of dynamite around an 18-inch pine tree. On a long fuse, they lit it and rushed away to hide behind a massive oak tree some 100 yards away. When the burning fuse hit the blasting cap, the pine tree base turned to wood chips and the tree fell directly on the camp.

The Duo waited for the shower of wood chips and splinters to stop before running to the outlaw camp. On arrival, two outlaws were crushed under the massive tree, two were speared to death and the other five were either unconscious or busy barfing from ruptured eardrums. All five living ones were secured with manacles. PF decided to go gather the remuda that had run off during the explosion, as Branch started gathering guns, saddlebags and pocket cash.

To his initial amazement, he collected $32,877 in currency. Separating $17.000 for the robbed ranchers and $9,000 for the balance due the bank—leaving $7,877. Unless someone had a known claim on part or all of that money, the Duo would keep it and not mention it to Sheriff Watkins. The Duo agreed to use these funds to help the dependents of the bank robbery victims after the bank settlement was disclosed.

For the next two days, the caravan of dead and living outlaws made its way back to Ellicott. To the Duo's surprise, Sheriff Watkins himself was waiting. It then took the entire next day to sell off the firearms, horses and collect the bounties via the telegraph service. With Sheriff Watkins payment of $1,000, and a $3,000 gift to a widow with two kids, The Duo and the sheriff left for Colorado Springs carrying the $17,000 for the ranchers and the Duo's new deposit of $22,000 for the Wells Fargo Bank of Colorado Springs.

*

The morning after arriving back at Colorado Springs, the Duo and the sheriff met at Georgiana's Diner for breakfast and a business meeting. Sheriff Watkins started, "well, you two have made a name for yourselves bringing in an army of 17 outlaws. The word gets around quickly in the lawmen circle, and that's why I just received a request from Sheriff Wilbur

Mondale in Limon. It seems that there is a gang of eight outlaws that have been robbing local banks in either Limon or Burlington. The three banks in Burlington have posted a $5,000 reward for the capture, dead or alive, of this gang. The four banks in Limon have matched this reward. So far $27,000 has been taken and three lives lost. Both sheriffs are asking for your help in capturing this gang. It's presumed that these outlaws have bounties on their heads as well."

Branch got the nod from PF and said, "we'll take the job. We'll be on the next train to Castle Rock and then switch to the eastbound train to Limon. If you were to notify Sheriff Mondale, we'll be there by tonight."

Arriving at the Limon depot, Sheriff Mondale was there to greet them. "Pick up your horses and I'll show you to your hotel and nearby livery. Then we'll get supper at Veronica's Diner."

After ordering their prime rib special, Sheriff Mondale started. "The Burlington banks have hired Pinkerton men to heavily guard their banks, so we expect that the bank robbery will now continue in Limon. To avert a financial catastrophe, two of the banks have closed their doors and their vault money transferred to the larger vaults in the Wells Fargo and Community banks. Now I, along with my two deputies, can guard the Community Bank if you two guys guard the Wells Fargo Bank."

PF added, "I suspect that everyone in town will know that the local law will be at the Community Bank and no one will be at the Wells Fargo."

"Correct, and yes, that is the best entrapment I can come up with. You men are capable of handling a gunfight, whereas, my deputies and I are not—truth be told. Besides, the big rewards go to those who take the biggest risks."

"Done. Tomorrow we'll meet with the local bank president and set up a scenario safe for employees."

*

President Taylor had been informed of the sheriff's plan. "Thank you for your willingness to help abort a bank robbery, so what do you have in mind?"

"How many employees work here, what time do they come to work, what time does the bank open, and what time is the vault open?" "Three clerks, one manager, and me. The bank opens at 9AM but the help gets here at 8AM to set up their cash and paperwork. The vault is open 8-9AM and after closing to store money overnight."

"Fine, the bank will likely be robbed between 8 and 9AM. From now on, send a teller with the greatest number of dependents home. I will be dressed as a teller but with my window temporarily closed. PF will be with you in your office to protect you. The bank president is always at greatest risk since he has the combination to the vault. When an outlaw crashes thru your door, PF will shoot him dead and then I'll let loose with my Mare's Leg. Just realize, the best laid plans don't always go the way you expect them, but we'll do our best to minimize collateral damage. I only ask that when the shooting starts, your two tellers are to crash immediately to the floor and not go for their pistol in their drawer. That would be a big mistake and their liability."

For the next three days, nothing happened. President Taylor was beginning to wonder if these precautions were warranted. On Thursday, the fourth day, all hell broke loose. Eight riders showed up wearing bandanas on their faces. Four stayed outside, one holding the horses' reins, two in the saddle guarding the east and west portion of Main Street, and the leader watching his crew from afar. Four outlaws broke the front door and rushed in. One outlaw stood by the door while the other three demanded where the bank manager was. Branch pointed to the president's office door as one man arched backwards and pounded his foot on the door. As the door opened, the outlaw recoiled into the door threshold, and caught a 44-40 caliber bullet in the chest. The two tellers collapsed to the floor, as Branch let go three deafening rounds. Two of the outlaws were blown over as the third, standing by the door, was blown backwards, over the porch, and into the outlaw horses. The outlaw holding the reins was thrown to the ground as the startled horse reared up and dumped him.

At that point, the gang's leader knew the robbery had been foiled, so he fired a pistol shot as a sign for his three outside men to retreat. The outlaws galloped out of town for three miles and then stopped to let their horses blow.

One outlaw asked, "what the hell happened, our man in town said the sheriff was at the Community Bank, so who was at Wells Fargo." "Must have been some hired Pinkertons or some bounty hunters. It doesn't matter, we're riding east, and we'll hop on the eastbound at the next water/coal station. We're going straight into Kansas and not stopping till we get to Dodge City some 300 miles from these gunfighters. I still have $25,000 from the bank heists, and we'll have some good living ahead in Dodge. So, let's ride all day before we set up camp."

Sheriff Mondale came to see the result of all that shooting. "Well, you got four of them, good for you. I'll look for some ID, match their faces with wanted posters, and collect their belongings. Are you going after the remainder of the gang?" "We sure are. I figure they will travel east to the first available train refueling stop which is 40 miles away. That means they'll set up camp tonight, and we'll visit them without an invitation, heh."

The Duo picked up their horses, including Buddy and some vittles, and took off at a slow trot. They were in no rush, they did not want to make a large dust cloud, nor did they want to get too close to the outlaws and face an ambush. Their goal was to visit their camp after the four were asleep.

As it happened, at 3AM, the Duo was standing in the middle of the outlaw camp. After wakening two outlaws and buffaloing them unconscious, they rolled them over and manacled them with their hands in their backs. Branch stepped up to another one, woke him up by touching his nose with the sawed-off shotgun. "You're going to rue the day if you try anything. Now roll over and put your hands in your back." With the manacles applied, PF did the same with the last outlaw.

With the four outlaws secured to trees, the Duo started a fire and cooked a full breakfast of canned potato home-fries, bacon, eggs, bread rolls and coffee. Rifling thru the outlaws' pockets and saddlebags, the Duo found $29,441. Separating $27,000 for the banks, the remainder of the cash was divided equally.

Arriving back in Limon late at night, the Duo left the outlaws with Sheriff Mondale; and the Duo had a home cooked meal followed by a bath and a restful sleep in a real hotel bed. Two days later, the Duo settled the finances with Sheriff Mondale. Following their usual distribution method, the settlement again awarded the Duo more money than any man had the right to have.

The Duo was having a leisurely dinner one day as Branch broached a sensitive subject. "Do you know how much money we have in our multiple bank accounts?" "I have some idea." "Well, to be specific, we have $70,000 each." "That is wrong. I have to confess that

50/50 distribution was not fair. So, I deposited some extra monies into your account. You have $90,000 and I have $50,000. And that's the way it should have been, and it will stay that way."

"Ok, if you insist. Now, you knew that I was making good my promise to a higher power. I believe that I am square. I also think it is time to walk away from bounty hunting and move to another profession. You see, in four weeks I am scheduled to enter the Lawman School in Denver for their four-month course. So, I think it is time for us to go our different ways."

"WHOA, SAY NO MORE. I have a second confession. You see, there is a Federal mandate to incorporate native Indians into the lawman workforce. Well, my tribe's Indian agent applied for me and I was accepted. The Indian agent has plans for me to become the reservation's chief of police. That still remains to be seen, but it is certain that I will be entering your class in one month." "Well, I'll be darned. When were you planning to tell me all this?" "I hadn't worked that out yet, but now that the cat is out of the bag, I feel so much better."

Without any warning, Sheriff Mondale plopped himself down at their table. "Before you say anything, let it be known that we are retiring from bounty hunting and going to the Lawman School in Denver." "Oh, I see, that's great. Actually, I was going to ask for a favor that is not about law and outlaws." "Well, in that case tell us about it."

"There is a pervert in town that is terrorizing Madame Hortense's House of Pleasure. This sadist is physically abusing the ladies and has to be convinced to cease his aberrant ways. I cannot arrest him since none of the gals want to file a complaint because they have been threatened with disfigurement. Would you consider speaking to Madame Hortense Willoughby before leaving town?" "Certainly, but no guarantees we can do anything about it either."

Hortense greeted the Duo in her Victorian parlor. "How may I be of service?" "We are here to talk to you, at the sheriff's request, about your customer with deviant sexual methods." "Well, step into my private office."

"What specifically is this man doing?" "He is inserting his fist and other objects in my ladies' private parts. Three of them have had stitches and are out of function." "Why don't they file charges and get this man arrested?" "Because he said that if they complained to the sheriff, he would disfigure them, and I don't meet facial damage." "What else is there to disfigure?" "He meant, cutting out their love button."

PF lost it and said, "Madame, we will visit this repulsive animal, and he won't be a problem ever again." "If you can do that for me, I will generously pay for your services."

On their way back to the hotel, Branch suggested they visit the local doctor who took care of the soiled doves. The visit was enlightening on the subject of "paraphilia," although the solution was a bit theoretical.

The next night, the Duo was waiting in hiding at the House of Pleasure. When Tyrone the pervert arrived, he requested Sally. Hortense went to tell Sally, but instead moved the Duo into Sally's room. As Hortense escorted him to her door, she stepped aside as Tyrone entered and closed the door. Hortense heard three thumps and a loud caterwauling as if Tyrone was in pain or shock. She smiled and walked away.

Inside the room, Branch had just placed three round-house punches to Tyrone's face, as PF had just pushed back Tyrone's right hand's second and third fingers till they both broke. "Now that we have your attention, we are going to cure you of your illness. It appears that you may have too much of that 'man hormone' called testosterone, which rhymes with Tyrone, heh?" PF shocks Tyrone by opening his fly and grabbing his scrotum. "Now we are going to geld you on one side—the side with the biggest oyster." "No-no-no" shaking his head sideways violently and foaming at the mouth.

PF pops the biggest oyster thru a small cut, and yanks it out with all the tubes and blood vessels. Tyrone screeched and then passed out. After reviving him PF said, "there you are, you can still use your tool and even enjoy relations, but hopefully in a normal sort of way with less of that testosterone flowing in your veins."

Branch continued, "now we expect you to be on the train tomorrow morning to Kansas. If you are not, we will find you and geld the other side. Will you be on the train in the morning?" "Yes-yes-yes" shaking his head up and down violently and foaming at the mouth. "Good, now give me $200 to pay for the gals medical bills and mental anguish. If I ever see your repulsive face again, it won't be pretty. "Now get out!" "Yes-yes-yes" while still foaming at the mouth.

The next day, the Duo took the train to Denver after witnessing Tyrone take the train to Kansas.

***

CHAPTER 5

Denver Days

The trip to Denver was covered in two hours. The first thing the Duo did was to find a livery for Chester and Hoss, but they left Buddy in another livery and sold him at a loss. It was now clear that Buddy's interest in the Duo's horses was not acceptable since the train's wrangler had confirmed Buddy's aberrant behavior while in the stock car.

With the entire month of August off, the Duo had time to get acquainted with the city. First and foremost, the Duo needed to find a place to live or would have to live in the dormitory and eat cafeteria food. Within a few days, they found a small two-bedroom house with a small barn and a three acre pasture some 1-2 miles from the Lawman School. During the school days, they could leave their mounts in the school's barn.

After buying the house and property for $2,250, they then proceeded to fill it with vittles and plenty of coffee. Realizing they were now living in a big city with a population approaching 100,000 people, they decided to put their cowboy clothes aside and buy citified duds. Also putting their pistol and sawed-off lever shotgun away, they each bought a Webley Bulldog with a shoulder holster.

During the month, they familiarized themselves with services located between their home and the school. They set up a bank account with the Wells Fargo Bank of Denver and had all their other accounts transferred to the one secure parent bank in Denver. They chose their favorite saloon and gambling casino as well as several mercantiles and hardware stores. Next to the school was the post office and several eateries. As huge as the city was, all their services were actually centrally located on

Willow Street without entering the city hubbub itself.

On Sept 1,1892, the Duo went to register for the four-month course. When the registrar found out they were proficient in firearms and tracking, he scheduled both with interviews. The two course instructors excused both from taking their classes based on experience, knowledge and demonstrated proficiency. In actuality, the Duo agreed to discuss their tracking experience and even agreed to assist the firearms instructor when teaching fast draw and point shooting. Getting back to the registrar with the signed instructor excuses, the Duo decided to take a modified meal plan for breakfast and dinner. Supper would be at home or in a local diner.

Commandant Peabody gave the introductory speech as he presented the subjects included in this course: Law, Firearms Training, Tracking, Self-defense, Safe Arrest Set-ups, and Jungle Warfare. At the end of his speech, he made it clear that of the students who pass the course, 95% would be offered a job working as a lawman in either Colorado or Texas.

Over the next four months, the Duo went thru the paces, even doing extra reading on the subject matter during the evenings at home. The law lectures included serving processes, organizing a trial, protecting judges and prosecutors, supervising executions, federal manhunts and more.

The Self-defense course emphasized avoiding being hit, disabling the opponent, making hits on the opponent count, and always be ready to kill an opponent that converts hand to hand combat to a mortal attack.

The lectures and demonstrations for safe arrests always emphasized having a man to cover your back. It described how to safely arrest an outlaw in a saloon, outdoor camp, or how to avoid an ambush on the trail. It especially emphasized how to equalize the odds in firepower and manpower before a confrontation. The basic safety mantra was, "Be wise, stay safe, for you need to fight another day."

Jungle Warfare was a new method used by old bounty hunters to demoralize, disable, and gain control of the killer outlaws. It included the most devious and eccentric methods and contraptions. Examples included: Trip wire booby traps, footwear nails, leg traps, predatory animals, poisoning food or liquor, and dynamite just to mention a few. This was the course where the students were encouraged to add their own warped personal ideas or contraptions—as the Duo eagerly demonstrated.

Of course, the Duo enjoyed assisting the instructors in the firearms and tracking courses. All in all, it was a very worthwhile four months training for a lifetime of work. A week before graduation, the school held a work fair. Any lawman in either Colorado or Texas was invited to the interviews. Every graduate's bio was given to all the visiting lawmen and interviews were arrange by Commandant Peabody. PF had two interviews scheduled with Sheriff Horskins of Waco Tx, and Sheriff McBain of Pueblo Co. Branch had one interview with Captain Ennis of the US Marshal Service.

After the interviews, the Duo went home to discuss options. PF discussed his interview with Sheriff Horskins. "He introduced himself as an older lawman who needed help with a town becoming lawless. He clearly said he needed a fast draw gunfighter who had sand. When confronted with my being a half breed, he quickly minimized the point. He was certain I was his man according to my recommendations from the lawmen we dealt with in the past year. My time spent with Sheriff McBain was nostalgic. He needed a second deputy but admitted that it was the Indian agent, from my tribes' reservation, that wanted me close by in Pueblo—a likely step to the reservation's Chief of Police."

"Wow, what a day. Sounds like the die is cast for Waco. I will miss you but realize you need to make your own way. Yet, my gut says we'll meet again. Now for me, I met the Captain, and he started the meeting by saying, "I received five recommendations on your behalf. Sheriff Watson of Durango, Sheriff McBride of La Junta, Sheriff McBain of Pueblo, Sheriff Watkins of Colorado Springs, and Sheriff Mondale of Limon. Now, quite simply, If I don't offer you a job, I would hate to walk the streets of Denver after nightfall. All kidding aside, these are all good lawmen, and I would be honored to offer The Mare's Leg Kid a position on one of our confrontational four-man squads in the position of gunfighter." "And the rest is history."

With PF heading to Texas, Branch bought out his half of the house, since Branch would need a home-base in Denver as a Colorado US Deputy Marshal.

*

The next two years went by like lightning. Branch had proven himself as a reliable protectant of his squad. Had been in several successful gunfights, had averted several ambushes on the trail, solved several murders, and proved to be the endless source of new jungle warfare. His moniker became well known and led to many living arrests of outlaws who would not challenge the Kid. Most important he had demonstrated the leadership qualities that is needed in a US Marshal's ability to function independently. When Captain Ennis had to choose one of his deputies to become a resident US Marshal in a lawless community, which had become a nidus of human trafficking, he knew who he had to call upon to serve the need.

Deputy US Marshal West arrived at Captain Ennis's office to meet with the boss. Branch realized that it was unusual for such an individual meeting, since every meeting he had attended in the past two years was with his squad for a new assignment.

*

"There is a major problem in southeast Texas. There is an underground system of transporting kidnapped women to Texas City next to Galveston. From there, they are transferred to ships heading for Mexico or points west in the Orient. We know the route used starts in Dallas, goes thru Waco, to finish in Texas City some 300+ miles away. It is presumed the distance is covered by train and by cross-country routes on horseback or by wagons. We've been trying to find an excuse to send a Marshal on site, but without looking suspicious, we've been on hold. A week ago the sheriff in Waco was gunned down during evening rounds by an alley footpad. Sheriff Horskins had been getting close to the known outlaws involved with the human trafficking and was likely killed for that reason. The shooter is known to the deputy sheriff, but needs help to break this kidnapping ring. He is asking for our help by sending a US Marshal to take over the office permanently."

"Were you to take this assignment, I would give you three able lawmen. The first is your old friend from your bounty hunting and lawman's training days. Yes, I'm referring to the one and only PF Silver. Officer Silver has made a name for himself. In two years he has earned the townsfolk's respect. He has had two gunfight confrontations with notorious outlaws. In one he put down two well-known outlaws and in the other, four men called out the sheriff and PF. The sheriff put one down with his shotgun while PF took out the other three. Since the sheriff's death, despite the townspeople's demands, the council has refused to make PF the sheriff because of their racial bias regarding his native blood. Of importance is the fact that PF suspects who the traffickers are, but he doesn't have the manpower to close their connections down."

"Well Captain, I would feel safe working with PF again. Who are the other two lawmen?" "The second is a retired marshal whose career ended with an honorable retirement just before you joined the force. The less you know about this man's identity, the safer our mole will be. Yes, he is our mole planted in Waco six months ago. The only person in town who knows who he is and how he is infiltrating the traffickers is PF Silver, himself." "What motive could an elderly man have to risk his peaceful retirement years?" "Because, he lost a cousin's daughter to this gang of altruistic outlaws. I may add, he is a good man with a gun, and you can trust him with your life. The only way you can make contact with him is to go to the Miner's Hammer Saloon, order a beer at the bar, and take your hat off to scratch your head. To be sure he noticed you, repeat the action after finishing your beer and leaving. You'll know it's him by the long white beard, old tan duster coat and the most beat up brown hat you'll ever see. He'll greet you with the words, 'howdy, you looking for your horse?' and you'll answer with 'yeah, he's a real dowager.' In case either of you forget the complete line, the certifying word is 'dowager.'"

"Most interesting, you really have prepared the path for the marshal's arrival. So, who is the third man." "Well, the third lawman is a woman!" "What, did you really mean that?" "I certainly did. Let me tell you the full story. The year after your graduation, federal funds were given to the Lawman School as long as at least one woman was added to every class. So we now have three gals entering the lawman's force. Most take secretarial jobs in our executive offices, but some join the work force as field operatives like yourself. The lawlady I'm referring to is born and raised in Waco, Texas."

"Oh really, it's beginning to sound like there is a real method to your madness. Please continue, you now have my total attention!"

'Well, this lady is aware that her town is a connecting location for the kidnapping trail to Texas City. She wants involvement and is even willing to go undercover by allowing herself to be kidnapped. In addition, she knows PF and would be honored to work with him as a deputy marshal."

"Great, now we have a potential team to consist of a half breed, an old codger, a woman and an outsider from Denver. Well I don't have to interview PF and I can't interview the codger who is 850 miles from here, but I can interview this lady before I make my decision."

"I wouldn't want any less than that, so let me tell you something about her. In Lawman School, she took the class first prize in self-defense and fast draw. She is a real looker and the most alert, determined, and astute woman I have ever met." As the Captain opened the door to his waiting room he said, "Marshal West, meet Deputy Marshal Gail Woods."

Branch stepped in the waiting room, as the lady stood up, they greeted each other by shaking hands. Gail added, "I'm pleased to meet you marshal, I've heard great things about you, and I would like to start by saying that I'm your huckleberry to put an end to human trafficking in my hometown." Branch was mesmerized and speechless, for way down deep he realized that no man on earth could ever escape the wiles of such a creation.

*

Captain Ennis realized that both participants were still holding hands and both staring at each other as if in some type of trance. So he chimed in, "now that you have officially met, why don't you all step into my office and have your interview. I have errands to run and will be back in an hour, heh?"

Branch stuttered something in agreement as he followed this new lawlady into the office and closed the door. Branch started, "could we use our given Christian first names instead of Marshal and Deputy Marshal? "Yes." "I'm Branch." "And I'm Gail." "What do you say that we present our bios till current times, and ladies first, heh?"

"Ok. I was raised on a horse ranch a mile from Waco. My dad and his brother owned the ranch till the fever hit our area and I lost both my parents and my aunt. My older sister and

I were raised by my uncle Otis who also ran the ranch. My sister went to school in Denver, married a lawyer and now resides in Denver. I was a ranch gal and grew up in the saddle. In school, I was more interested in raising horses and learning how to run the business. After high school graduation, I worked along with Uncle Otis till he decided I needed higher learning. He sent me to Denver to live with my sister and attend business school. During that first year of accounting and business management, my best friend and I got interested in pistol fast draw. We joined a local shooting club that specialized in fast draw. At the end of our year, we changed our major to law. Becoming a lawyer was not our destiny, so we both applied to the Lawman School and were accepted. And that brings us up to this meeting."

"Very interesting background. I'm afraid my bio is much more mundane. But here goes. Raised in Durango, the son of a miner. I tried underground mining, but failed miserably because of claustrophobia. Worked in a gun shop for a while and learned how to repair guns.

Because of an old school injury, I could not learn fast draw with a pistol, so the gunsmith set me up with a lever action Winchester shotgun. I learned how to master the firearm and eventually became a bounty hunter with PF Silver. During a year's time we amassed a large bank account. PF used the money to feed his family and tribe, as I started a benefactor fund to help the dependent victims of crimes. Afterwards, we both joined the Lawman School. For two years, PF has been the deputy sheriff in your town, and I became a US Marshal assigned to a confrontational group. It seems I've been all over Colorado on assignments. After living in Colorado all my life, I'm now ironically offered a resident job in Texas. And this brings us to today."

Gail added with a smile, "but you skipped the fact that you earned a moniker, 'The Mare's Leg Kid,' for sure?" "Well, I learned from PF a long time ago, that self-aggrandizing has a way of eventually working against you, heh?"

"Do you mind if I ask you some poignant questions regarding the work of a lawman?" "Not at all, go ahead and don't hold back."

"Good, how are you going to deal with the prim and proper who feel that it isn't acceptable for a lady to be working or seen with men without a chaperone." "Being a horse woman all my life, I've had to deal with the hypocrites and I no longer let the societal niceties control my life."

"Good, have you ever killed a man, and do you think you could?" "No, I haven't and will only know when the time comes. All I know is that I'm committed to perform my duties, and have no qualms in doing what is needed to preserve my life and the life of my partners."

"Again, good. You're aware that an educated female wearing a gunfighting rig is quite intimidating to men." "I look at it this way, I'm not a yokel and proud of it. I also don't flaunt my education. Like most women, I also want to find a man, but upholding the law and putting an end to human trafficking is now my priority."

"Great, well please don't be offended, but I've been avoiding the real issue. My real reservation is well, how do I say this? Uh well, even if I stretch my imagination, you're no 'booglin!'" "What on earth is a booglin?" "Short, fat and ugly!" "Oh, well I guess that's a compliment." "Let me be frank, you are one heck of a beautiful woman with all the female attributes in the right sizes. How on earth are outlaws going to deal with you?"

Silence followed as Gail added, "I see, well I could color my hair blonde, start prattling like an idiot, chew tobacco and spit at the outlaws, drink rotgut whiskey, flatten my attributes with a corset and wear a duster to hide my bum. Heck remember that even Calamity Jane could look like an ill kept drunk but still was a woman who loved men." "I see, well we'll work on it. Now, it's your turn. Do you have any questions?"

"Yes, are you willing to treat me as an equal?" "I have every intention to do so and I know PF will feel the same way. If I come across any differently, I would expect you to call me out." "Good, did I appear sassy with my answers?" "No, it's clear you are a bright and a self-assured individual. The Captain said you were astute and that fits you well." "That's it for me. My future is in your hands"

"In that case, I would be very comfortable in asking you to join our team and head back to Waco on the next train." "I accept without reservations." "Great, and would you honor me by accompanying me to the Denver Princess Hotel for supper. I look forward to hearing about your horse ranch." "I would like that very much, for sure! Shall we say 6PM at my sister's home at 12 Waters Street." "I'll be there by taxi."

*

Dressed in his best official uniform and wearing his US Marshal Badge and a Bulldog under his vest, he made his way to 12 Waters in a local taxi. Stepping on the porch, he knocked and waited. A young lady with family resemblances appeared. "Hello, Marshal West, I'm Cindy and Gail is waiting for you in the parlor, please come in." Stepping in the parlor was Cindy's husband, Carl Crimshaw, who stepped to shake Branch's hand. "Nice to meet you Marshal. Branch heard nothing as he spotted Gail standing nearby. She was ravishing in a straight one-piece blue dress with well-placed jet-black hair and a gorgeous smile to boot. "Good evening Gail, this is a pleasant surprise to get to meet your family." "Well now you've met them, and I suspect your taxi is waiting. Shall we go, I'm famished." "Certainly, after you ma'am."

Once in the taxi, Gail said, "boy, you really sounded official with that awful word, Ma'am." Well, for your family's appearance, I thought the word fit well, but we're back to Gail and Branch. By the way you look exquisite in that dress, and I'm certainly glad you didn't appear in that awful disguise you described today." As both broke out in laughter.

Small talk got them to the Princess Hotel. Branch stepped down first and as Gail was to step down, she hesitated because of her tight dress. Gail added, "I know this is not modest, but I have no choice, either I raise my dress, or you carry me down off this carriage." "Pull it up and think nothing of it." She did so, but Branch ended up arching his eyebrows.

Walking into the hotel lobby revealed a Victorian décor that was an eyeball overload. The restaurant itself was more opulence than imaginable. Branch informed the maître-dee that he had a reservation for Marshal West and a deputy. The maître-dee asked if a third person would be joining them and Branch chortled and added, "no, the lady is my deputy." The maître-dee, realizing his blunder, added his own chortle and simply seated them at a table for two.

Settling in, Gail added, "I guess we'll have to get used to that surprise look. So, do we spend the evening talking about life and lawlessness in Waco, or do we talk about horse ranching as you hinted at today." "In two days, we'll have 850 miles to cover from Denver to Waco. We'll have almost 24 hours to talk business. Let's talk about your ranch and your life's work over a beer or wine." "I prefer a beer since I never developed the taste for wine." "Done, we have all evening, so let's put off ordering our meal. Please tell me about your ranch."

"We raise two lines of horses. The 'American Quarter Horse' for riding and medium duty work and the 'Belgian Draft Horse' for heavy work. The Quarter Horse has a calm disposition, is heavily muscled, has a short body, is agile, and is smart with a pleasant personality. Functionally, this breed can ride all day, break sod, work cattle, pull wagons and race. They are incredible short distance sprinters on a quarter mile course. The racing component is my uncle's hobby, as horse pulling with Belgian's is, but they are not high-income producers."

"Knowing the different color coats, how do you keep the lines pure?" "Yes, my uncle wrestled with the +-dozen colors to include" sorrel, chestnut, bay, black, white, palomino, pinto, dun, grulla, buckskin, and roan—and all with or without black points." "Whoa, what are black points?" "Oh, the black hair on the tail, lower legs, mane, and ear edges."

"Wow, now you're dealing with a total of 24 combinations and even worse with cross breeding." "Yes, my uncle recognized the problem years ago and found the solution. We only breed and raise sorrels, chestnuts, and bays. These three colors are very similar and are the standards of unmarked horses. No one wants to ride a marked horse such as a black, white, pinto, and all the other identifiable coat colors. That way we keep only three colors of stallions and we do not cross breed."

"To be more specific the sorrel's coat is red/copper. If it has points, they are blonde or flaxen. The chestnut is a wine or brownish red coat with either natural or flaxen points. The Bay has a brown body with black points. Now you know why we call them unmarked colors." "Amazing, now tell me a bit about the Belgian Horse."

"Now that is an amazing huge but gentle animal. It is in high demand today because the farmers used to have a plow with one blade, then two was better and now three is the best. Consequently, our work geldings cannot handle the new 'improved' cultivating tools, so the draft work horse, even more expensive than a work gelding, is in high demand. Ironically, we also have the same three coat colors as the Quarter horse. These are short, stocky, and muscular pullers with a kind temperament and easy to handle. Unlike our work geldings measuring up to 17 hands and weighing up to 1,200 pounds, the Belgians can be up to 19 hands and weigh in the realm of 2,000 pounds."

"How many horses do you have?' "We have 150 Quarter horses and 50 Belgian draft horses." "How big is your ranch and how is the acreage separated?" "The ranch is three sections or nearly 2,000 acres. One hundred acres is cultivated for hay, fifty acres for straw and six hundred acres are now pastured, partitioned, and fenced. As you can see, with plenty of water, we can expand our operations. As far as buildings, the ranch house has four bedrooms and is a beautiful home. The horse barn has fifty stalls and we have a separate hay/straw barn. We have a twelve-bed bunkhouse with a cook shack/dining area. We have eight full time employees which includes two trainers, a cook, a harness maker, a foreman, a blacksmith/farrier, a wrangler, and a horse whisperer."

"Well, that is an impressive business and you've been talking a heck of a chin-wag without stopping. Maybe we should order and then we can talk some more over coffee after our supper."

"Fine, let's order and while we wait for our food, you can tell me why you're so interested in our ranch."

Looking at the menu, it was clear that this wasn't going to be a meat and potato meal with apple pie as a dessert. Gail said, "looks like we're going to have at least several courses— appetizer, soup, salad, fruit to clear the palate, entrée with vegetables, flambé dessert and a side of bread and coffee/tea. I guess, this is what is called a seven-course meal, for sure?" Branch was somewhat ill at ease as he asked Gail to order for him, She never missed a step and ordered brie cheese as appetizer, a cup of hot potato soup, an iceberg slice with oil/vinegar dressing, sliced oranges as palate cleanser, an entre of Chateaubriand with buttered/sour cream baked potatoes and carrots, and a dessert of flambé caramel flam.

Fortunately, the courses came in stages with plenty of time to provide small talk between courses. After the medium-rare tenderloin entrée, there was a welcomed rest before the dessert. "Well, that was a great meal. I have to confess that I did not know what a Chateaubriand was, but I was pleased to see a tenderloin steak arrive with all the fixings."

"Now it's your turn, why the apparent interest in raising horses or were you just easing into a conversation?" "My interest is genuine. Have you ever heard of the AA ranch in Pueblo?" "Why of course, Anson Aiken was a good friend of my dad. Why do you mention his ranch?" "Because some time ago, I put a deposit on one colt and two fillies. They had the right lineage and PF selected the horses as likely good sprinters. I have three more months before I take possession or ask for a 50% refund on my investment."

"How much was the deposit?" "It was $2,000 per animal, and if the animal ran ¼ mile in 20-22 seconds, another $1,000 will take the horse to my ranch. If any horse did not clock the 20-22 seconds, I would get my money back, or take the horse for breeding stock without any more money down." "You made a heck of a deal. I'm sure that Anson Aiken is hoping you want your money back, since if they clock in the 20-22 second range, they are worth $5,000 each even if unproven in a race." "So where is your ranch?" "Don't have one yet, but I suspect I'll buy some land around Waco since I'm going to be stationed there, heh?" "Good idea, for sure!"

After lingering till closing time, Branch paid the bill, and the couple exited the Hotel to take a curbside taxi. Standing on the porch, the doorman called a taxi up. As Gail was about to pull her dress up to climb the taxi's steps, the doorman appeared holding a hand tarp up to cover Gail's exposed legs. Branch simply arched his eyebrows up, but in reality, he wanted to trounce the doorman for stealing his view.

The short trip to Gail's family home was marked by silence since the evening had come to an end. At their destination, the driver also appeared with that damned hand tarp to maintain the lady's modesty. Branch made the mental note to use a public taxi next time and avoid the high-end methods of the rich and famous.

Standing on the porch, Branch said, "It was a great evening and I'd say we did not waste the moment. On that note, I leave you to pack and I'll pick you up at 9AM in two days." Branch doffed his hat, stepped back and said goodnight.

*

Gail walked inside and ran into Cindy and Carl who had their ear to the front door. Cindy asked, "well, what do you think of him?" "He is a gentleman, determined, goal motivated, somewhat a winsome. Oh hell, that's the man I'm going to marry, but he don't know it yet."

The next day Branch went to a gun shop and purchased a 44 Bulldog and a 41 derringer. He then stopped at a mercantile and purchased several carpetbags to hold all his earthly belongings. After packing, he thought of stopping to see Gail, but decided to hold back since it was too presumptive on his part. As he sat on the hotel porch rocking away, he thought, *"this woman has had a profound effect on my mind. She is beautiful, alert, bright, sassy, astute, comely, witty, easy to talk to, loves horses and I need to find the perfect bait because she's a real catch. Actually, she don't know it yet, but*

I'm going to marry her. Meanwhile, we'll be working together in a dangerous profession and we mustn't let our emotions cloud our thinking."

*

Two days later, Branch had purchased a stock tag for Chester with hay and oats, and two tickets with all meals and Pullman berths for comfort. As they were situated in the passenger car, Branch finally noticed what Gail was wearing. She had on a presumed lady's typical uniform of a blue hickory shirt, fitted riding skirt, grey vest, grey hat, cowboy boots and her Colt Model 1878 in a cross draw. When Branch asked her why she was using a cross draw she said, "women have wide hips and small narrow waists. That makes a pistol grip hit the side of the body and fast draw is not possible. I tried to wear my gunbelt on my hips, but that makes it impossible to sit in a saddle."

After some small talk, Branch presented his goals. First, we have to clean up the town of malevolent and known outlaws. That will mean several arrests and confrontations in the saloons. Secondly, we need to make contact with our mole and start tearing up the kidnapping trail." They talked and prepared a system of going from one saloon to another, while using PF's photographic memory. After several hours, dinner was served in the dining car and the Duo took a break.

After dinner, Branch said, "yesterday, I went shopping and bought you several things. First, here are novels by Swanson and Harrison on bounty hunting and marshaling. It includes what men do when they retire from living by the gun. Also, when you don't have your colt, always carry in your dress pocket or reticule, this double action 5-shot Webley Bulldog in 44 caliber. Along with either of your pistols, always carry this two-shot derringer in 41 caliber. One day, either pistol will save your life."

"Guess we were both thinking of keeping occupied, so I went to the bookstore and bought two books. The one for you is 'Everything you need to know to raise work and riding Quarter horses.'" "And what did you get for yourself?" "A book on something I know nothing about, as she sheepishly takes the book out of her carpetbag and reads, 'Everything you need to know to raise and race Quarter horses.'" As both broke out in all out laughter.

Over the next 24 hours, the Duo read, ate, napped, talked and slept all night in their individual berths. They did a lot of talking about horses, family life and the stress in upholding the law, but whatever the subject, neither was ever at a loss for words. Without either realizing it, they were bonding as a couple before any physical contact.

On the last leg of their trip, Gail fell asleep in her seat. As the train lurched at the Waco train station, Gail awoke to almost find herself half crawled all over Branch. Branch spoke, "well that was a nice nap, and while you were sleeping, I finished both books on Quarter horses. I have several questions that you can clarify for me sometime over supper. But for now, it's time to face the music. We are now in Waco and this could be the beginning of our destiny, heh?" "For sure!"

***

CHAPTER 6

Cleaning up Waco

Stepping on the platform, PF came up, shook Branch's hand, and said, "you're a sight for a frustrated deputy sheriff. I had no idea you were the one Captain sent until yesterday." PF then got a slap on the shoulder as Gail said, "and what am I, chopped liver?" "Lady, it's been two long years without your presence, and now, look at you, a Deputy Marshal. I'm totally amazed," as he takes Gail in a full body hug.

Branch then asked, "where do we start?" PF then took over. "Otis will meet us around 5PM at the Waco General Hotel. Today, he has several doctor visits for his rheumatism. So, we have all afternoon to get you up to snuff. Let's bring your luggage to your rooms at the General, and then we'll meet at the office for privacy."

Later, after the first of several coffee pots, PF started. "Since Sheriff Horskins' death, several gangs have seemingly dropped out of the proverbial 'outlaw ugly tree.'" "Why is that?" "Because, they know I won't challenge them without a backup—the number one rule in making arrests in a crowd." Gail added, "well, how many saloons will we have to clean out before these pinheads get the message?" "At least five and one gambling casino." Branch added, "we'll start tomorrow by walking the streets for people to notice us, and we'll get acquainted with some of the merchants and banks. Tomorrow night, we start cleaning up the saloons. So, let's spend some time reviewing the wanted posters. I'm sure they are all stored in your photographic brain, heh?" "Yes sir, and several will get retired tomorrow night, I say!"

"Now, where are we with human trafficking?" "Our mole, who goes by the name of Pappy, is a well-known patron of the 'Miner's Hammer Saloon' and he lives in Maude's Boarding House.

As of yesterday, he knew the name of the three men who were managing the 'hostage house' where they hold their victims coming in from Dallas. Pappy's been used to bring three gals to the next 'hostage house' somewhere in College Town, some 90 miles from here. He wants to hold up on raiding them till he finds out where the hostage house is located in Waco." Gail had a thought, "seems likely, when we raid two hostage houses in Waco and College Town, that Pappy's cover will be exposed, and he'll be on his way back to Denver."

Branch then added, "well, it's 4:30 and I guess we should head for the General." PF asked that they start their visit with Otis while he did his afternoon rounds when most merchants closed up and went to the banks with their daily deposits. By PF walking around, it discouraged footpads from attempting to steal the daily deposits. PF would join them by 6:30 for supper.

Walking down the boardwalk for several blocks, Branch accidentally touched Gail's hand. Before either realized it, they were holding hands. As they entered the General Hotel's parlor, Otis was already there and noted the hand holding. Without a pause, Gail jumped in the arms of a frail white-haired gentleman. "Gosh little girl, you look more mature every time I see you." "And that was six months ago last summer." "Are you really here to stay, this time?" "Yes, Otis. This is where I've always wanted to be. Oh, excuse me, uncle, this is Marshal Branch West, the new head lawman in town and my boss." After proper introductions, the three were headed for the restaurant, when Branch excused himself to go register and pay for three rooms.

While Otis and Gail were waiting to be seated Otis said, "we need to talk business finances, do we do it in front of the marshal or do we wait? Otis, this man will be my husband soon, although he doesn't know it yet. I think you can say anything you want, since I'm not about to start hiding things from him." "Well, we're all set, we have three rooms for the night—and yes, one for your uncle who is not going to travel alone at night, heh?" "For sure!"

After being seated, Otis started, "I have had a tough month with my rheumatism. I spent all day seeing four doctors, getting blood tests and many pictures of my hands and especially my deformed fingers. The consensus of these four doctors is that I have a disabling form of rheumatism called rheumatoid arthritis. The long and short of this is that I am in a lot of pain and eventually, I will have many of my joints destroyed by this arthritis." "What can the doctors do to treat this condition?" "In Waco, nothing. They want me to go see a specialist in Denver who is getting marvelous results with a new expensive medication. The catch is that he insists on seeing these patients every three days, which I cannot do from Waco."

Gail jumps in and says, "so you temporarily move in with Cindy and get the medical care you need." "That is my goal, but for one thing. I just can't continue to run the ranch, I need to sell it, take my share of the money and move to Denver permanently for long term medical care or I'll be an invalid within months." "Ok, how do we do it, because I want to own it." "I knew you would say that, so let's go over the finances."

"The business as it is set up now, with all business expenses paid, an improvement account funded, and all your personal, frivolous, and household expenses covered, you can put $1,500 in the bank yearly of pure profit. Since this is a going concern that demands a business top price, let's break down the cash and assets. In the past 15 years, I have amassed a cash savings account of $20,000. For assets we have horses, buildings, supplies, land, and agricultural equipment. The value is:

200 horses at $150 = $30.000
Buildings and supplies = $5.000
Agricultural equipment = $2,000
3 sections of land=1,920 acres = $2,000
Fenced in pastures/paddocks = $1,000
                TOTAL ASSETS = $40,000

There was silence as each one was thinking. It was Otis who broke the ice by saying, "so if you get half the savings, you now have half of your $20,000 payment to own the ranch lock stock and barrel." Gail was next to speak, "the numbers look simple enough, but which bank in Texas will lend $10,000 to a woman?" Otis retorted, "that is our dilemma, but I need this money to move to Denver and pay for my exuberant medical care."

Silence again. Branch then spoke for the first time. "What I'm about to say and do is very clear to me. So, for a $20,000 bank loan, Gail gets full ownership and keeps half of the savings account for guaranteed operational expenses?" "Absolutely." Branch opens his vest, grabs a booklet, and starts writing. Tearing off the paper, he hands Otis a bank draft for $20,000. Branch adds, "I'm certain Wells Fargo will honor the draft, and Miss Woods, we'll sign a promissory note later, heh?" Gail exploded, "WHOA there you all. Branch West, OUTSIDE." As she gets up, grabs Branch's hand and drags him out of the restaurant, thru the parlor and outside on the boardwalk. PF was not seen, but was nearing the hotel when he saw Gail aggressively drag Branch outside and a serious discussion appeared to ensue. He hid around a building and watched.

Standing in a firm akimbo stance, and with a rather decisive voice, Gail said, "Mister West, what are you up to?" "Well Miss Woods, I just had an epiphany and saw my destiny in front of me. Can't you see what is happening?" Abandoning her akimbo stance, and in a rather soft soothing contralto voice she added, "I think I do, but please make it clear to me, for sure."

"Ok, after Otis spoke, I saw a woman, that I have uncertain feelings for, who was teetering on the verge of losing the dream of her life."

"Stop, you have feelings for me?"

"After spending the last three days with you, I want to get to know you better. I'm feeling a strong attraction to you and I don't know if it's simply lust, or the real thing. One thing is for sure, If I am going to live only one more day, I want it to be with you. Am I overreading you or how do you feel about me?"

Gail took her hands off her hips, brought them to her face and started crying. "During these three days, I thought I was going to go crazy. I was feeling strange urges that I never experienced before. What was worse, I did not dare express my feelings since I was afraid I was just experiencing an infatuation. Every day my feelings accentuated to the point that I now yearn for you. So where do we go from here?"

"We go into business together. We are marshals and have a job to do as we are now business partners in a horse ranch—which I know very little about and have a lot to learn, heh?" "For sure, then what?"

"Then we let nature take its course. I hope that our attraction will become a commitment and we'll hopefully fall in love."

Gail nodded yes as Branch approached her and gently kissed her. After separating, Gail wanted more. They came back together in a lustful contact, but as the two began to settle down, their embrace became a profound passionate union. Eventually, after separating, Gail said, "oh, my." Branch added, "yeah, that kiss had a clear message, heh?" "For sure!"

"I think we had better go back inside, Uncle Otis will begin to think we absconded. At that point, PF arrived. "I say, that was a good show, I heard nothing but saw everything. I recall an old family saying, "when a man and woman commit to each other, no one should contest the event. I am proud to be the first to support and congratulate you."

Getting back to their table, Otis had not touched the bank draft. Gail took the draft and handed it to her uncle. "The deal is good and yes; Branch is my significant other—as she took Branch's hand and broke into the biggest smile Otis had ever seen.

Otis was clearly satisfied with the outcome when he saw that Gail was so happy. Gail then asked if their foreman, Gary Ashburn was capable of running the business till she could be free of her commitment to Waco and the kidnapped women. "Of course, he's been doing that for six months while I spent most of my days in bed or in a rocking chair."

After a fine supper, the people went their own way and Otis agreed to meet the next morning at the town clerk to transfer the deed, and the bank to transfer the account in Gail's name.

That evening, the lovers met in Gail's room to say goodnight. The kissing progressed to fondling and both realized that it would soon reach a point of no return. They stopped, but both knew that this was just the beginning, their next encounter would be more intimate, and mutual familiarity would bring an assurance of their commitment.

The next morning, Otis signed over the deed to Gail and after withdrawing his $10,000, he opened his own private account with a new deposit of $30,000. When Gail offered to sign a partnership agreement instead of a promissory note, Branch agreed to the agreement but clarified, "money is not important here, your feelings toward me are of the essence and I know how you feel. But as a realistic life insurance, we should both be legal partners and each the primary beneficiary of the partnership in the event one of us passes away." In case both partners pass away, Gail's secondary beneficiary would be PF Silver and Branch's would be his parents. To accomplish all the legalities, the Duo went to see an attorney to prepare the contract and beneficiaries.

With the paperwork done, the Duo picked up PF at the office and went on midday rounds. Gail personally introduced Branch to the merchants they carried a ranch account with. She made it clear that he was co-owner with all the rights needed to conduct business. Included were: Jed Barber of Jed's gun shop, Sam and Edna Washburn's Mercantile, Josh Martin telegrapher, Roger Whitmore's Hardware, Goodson's leather products, Cramer's Iron Works, Burton's Feed and Seed, Doc Harris veterinarian, Porter Henderson postmaster, and the Doctor's Hospital-Doc Ross and Sims.

That night, they agreed to meet PF and start arresting outstanding outlaws as part of their cleaning the town of deplorables.

*

Before walking into the Blue Moon saloon to arrest a gang wanted for bank robbery and murder, Branch set up the Trio's positions. "I will be the one to address the outlaws and both of you are my backup standing behind me on my right and left. Watch out for patrons who enter the confrontation without warning. If there is a shootout, you are responsible for the one outlaw on your side. I'm responsible for the balance in the center of the group. The only other important things are to make sure the bartender is no longer armed with that shotgun under the bar and there is no one entering thru the batwing doors with a gun in hand. Any questions?" With none, "good, let's go in."

As they entered, they drew their guns as Branch yells out, "Cletus Piscan, stand up and put your hands up. I'm Marshal West and you're under arrest for murder." As Cletus stands, Branch looks at the other three men at the same table and says, "you three dickheads follow suit, now." As all four outlaws were standing and facing the Trio, not a one had put his hands up. It looked as all four were waiting for someone. BANG. Gail had just fired a shot at a man in the saloon who was standing with his gun cocked and pointed at Branch. The surprise shooter was hit between the eyes and with the neural impact, he had flailed his arms up and fired his pistol harmlessly at the wall as he collapsed to the sawdust floor.

Several of the patrons were covered with gore as Branch sensed a gunfight was about to happen. "Everybody, clear out of here, now. That includes you bartender. Well Cletus, now that your ambush is foiled, what's it going to be. Surrender, or die tonight. And you men, the same option is yours as well. Might be wise to try your luck with a good lawyer and go for a prison sentence. Who killed that teller anyways?" Cletus' eyes changed and he went for his gun. Branch shot once and blew Piscan across the table with a hit high on the chest. The rest of the outlaws put their hands up and surrendered.

Little did any of the marshals realize that two patrons were watching the Trio at work. Pappy, the old white bearded underground codger with a crushed brown hat who made no attempt to hide himself from PF. The other was a scar faced rude character by the name of Dirty Dick Banks, who was looking at Gail salaciously while hiding behind a furtive look.

PF had already collected the living and dead outlaw's cash totaling $187. Gail collected all the pistols and gunbelts as Branch asked the barkeep how much to clean up the gore and cover the undertaker fees. "My name is Horace and $10 should do it as long as the next time you make an arrest in my saloon, remember that I want to join forces and help you out?" "Ok Horace, we'll remember that."

By the time the three outlaws were escorted to jail, it was almost approaching 1AM. PF suggested that they call it a night, since the word of tonight's arrest would already have cleared the other saloons of the miscreants that would return in a few days. "See you tomorrow and If I need you before noon, I'll find you. It will take me a half day to get bounty rewards, and sell the outlaw horses and firearms."

As the Duo was walking back to their hotel, Branch asked if Gail was Ok with the shooting. "You saved my life tonight, since I had not seen that hidden fifth man. Are you that sure of yourself to shoot a man between the eyes, and are you ok with killing a man?"

"That outlaw was about to shoot you, and I wasn't going to let that happen. Besides that was an easy shot for me to make. And yes, I'm ok to shoot an outlaw who wants to kill us at all costs. If there is one phrase I will never forget is the one spoken by Commandant Peabody and Captain Ennis, you know, if an outlaw.........it's time to kill or be killed."

Arriving at their hotel, Branch escorted Gail to her room. Once inside, Gail took his hand and walked him to the settee. There they held each other and started kissing. "Do you have to leave; I want us to become more intimate and that doesn't mean sleeping in separate rooms." "I want the same, but I'm afraid that we won't be able to control our emotions." "Well, that wouldn't be such a bad thing, for sure. So, when you're ready, I'll be here for you. Now kiss me and get out before my urges take over." "Yes, Miss Woods, see you in the lobby at 8AM and we'll go to Millie's Diner for breakfast."

*

Gail arrived in the parlor only to find Branch already waiting. Branch, got up, gave Gail a loving kiss and asked how she had slept. "On and off in fits longing for you." "I just paid and canceled my room. My stuff will be moved to your room. I see no reason why we can't sleep together. Besides, I cannot imagine spending another sleepless night wanting to be with someone—ever again!" Gail simply took his hand and walked outside.

Arriving at Millie's Diner, the Duo ordered coffee and asked for some time to talk. "I thought last night, how we could cover a subject on horse ranching every morning before doing lawman's work." "Great idea, what is the subject for today?" "Feeding horses and raising crops." "Good, I'll start and stop me if you have any questions."

"There are two locations for feeding horses, stalled or pastured. A stalled adult horse weighing 1000 pounds eats 2 pounds of hay per 100 pounds of weight, or 20 pounds per day per adult horse. Since a 50 lb. bale of hay has

12 flakes of separated hay, then each flake is roughly 4 lbs. and it will take 5 flakes a day to feed the adult horse separated in two feedings morning and night. Along with the hay, the adult horse also gets a 3.5 lb. bait of oats twice a day. At midday, we feed them 4-6 pounds of straw."

"Why three feedings a day, that is really new to me!"

"Horses have small stomachs and bile is continually added to the stomach, not stored and released during a meal. Multiple feedings is the best method of feeding them. The straw is low in energy and requires a lot of chewing which is what horses like to do. Along with the hay, oats and straw, horses need 5-10 gallons of water per day and 1-2 ounces of salt."

"What is the nutrient value of this feed" "Hay is low in carbohydrates and high in protein, fiber, vitamins and minerals as long as we feed cultivated and seeded hay, to include timothy, tall fescue and brome grass that does well in Texas. Oats is a perfect grain for all horses because of a nice distribution between starch, fiber, protein, and fat. Straw is mostly fiber and low calories. We also use straw in horses that are heavy eaters or horses not working or riding for long periods."

"Now pastured horses are a different matter. A horse cropping meager grasses on the range will forage 17 hours a day and likely end up eating 20-25 pounds of pasture vegetation. This feed is low in calories and supplements. When it is really hot in the summer, we bring horses out of the sun and feed them. At dusk, they resume foraging."

"In the winter, horses continue to forage and eat grasses that are dead, dormant or the result of fallow land. These horses are supplemented with hay. There are other groups of horses that need supplementation year-round, and often with specialized feed pellets. These include pregnant mares, foals, growing horses and hard-working horses—gelded quarter horses and draft horses."

"Wow, you are a fund of knowledge, and it's nice to see that your words match the textbook you gave me. Now, let's have breakfast, and afterwards, we'll talk about raising crops to feed your horses." Gail ordered first and asked for steak and eggs with toast and pan-fried potatoes. Branch said, "ditto."

"Now, tell me how you can eat like that and still maintain your slim figure!" "Well, I wasn't raised on clabber and I enjoy my food. The truth be told, after breakfast, I don't eat till the evening supper and only then in moderation." After their meals arrived, the Duo ate in relative silence. Afterwards, over another pot of coffee, Branch asked, "please tell me about the crop portion of this ranch."

"There are two reasons we raise crops: feeding and training horses. First, let's discuss feeding horses year-round, intermittently or as a supplement."

"You recall the 20 lbs. of hay a horse can eat in a day, now multiply that by 90 days, the standard winter season. That comes of 1800 pounds of hay, say a ton for simplicity. Now we cultivate, seed and fertilize 100 acres of quality hay. This yields 2 tons per acre in two crops, or 200 tons of hay. Since a horse needs one ton per winter, then the 200 tons will feed our 200 horses, and the straw and grain is extra, heh? Now this is in theory since we rarely feed horses all winter. We feed them on and off and basically supplement them. So that is why we always have a hay surplus for sale to cattle ranchers, heh?" "For sure, now you have me using your saying and you using mine."

"So in order to grow the size of your herd, we need to cultivate more land for oats and hay." "Absolutely, we have the land and that's not the problem. Money is the problem. Now will you start saying our herd and not your herd."

"Yes, that would be nice, but under one condition." "That is." "That money will not be an issue if it is spent on our behalf, heh? Now what did you mean about growing crops being used to train horses?"

"Think about it, we sell work horses. Did you really think horses are born with the natural ability to pull a plow, a mower, or even a simple wagon. Harness training is done by our trainers, who use the old method of matching a trained horse with an untrained one to do field work. Over time every horse is used with all the agricultural equipment from plowing to baling and delivering hay." "So which came first, the need to feed horses or the need for harness training them to farming equipment?" "It was a mutual need."

"My last question is somewhat speculative. Is there any money to be made in selling hay." "Yes, take the 100 acres that yields 200 tons in two crops. A bale of hay weighs 50 lbs. and that means that 40 bales makes a ton, or 200 tons equals 8,000 bales. At 75 cents a bale that the ranchers are paying to get hay here by train, your 8,000 bales are worth $6,000. Deduct the yearly labor and the depreciated agricultural equipment, and I'd say you would still be left with a sizeable profit of at least $3,500, for sure! Doing this, you might need to build another hay barn and a pull thru shed to store the farming machinery."

"Well that does it for today. Let's go see PF and see how he's doing trying to peddle the outlaw goods, checking on bounties and how he's arranging for Judge Hobart from Austin to come to Waco, or for the accused to be delivered to Austin for a trial."

Finding PF on the porch sunning himself, he proudly said that we had hit a jackpot. "I sold the horses with saddles for $450, the 10 firearms for $300, and the bounties came to $3,000. Divided by three equals $1,250 each." "Not quite, you're using bounty hunting distribution, this is US Marshal distribution. $750 for horses and firearms goes to Captain Ennis, that's what he uses to pay for your wages, medical and disability insurance, for sure, heh!" "Simple, we all still get $1,000 a piece, I say!"

While contemplating doing morning rounds, suddenly Sam Washburn arrived at a huff. "Marshals, two mercantiles have been robbed of an estimated $10,000 in cash from Bowman's and Wadsworth's Mercantile." Branch adds, why do mercantiles carry that much cash in their store safes?" "Because the banks close at 5PM whereas the mercantiles are open till 8PM. And of course, during the day, a steady supply of customers makes it difficult to take the time to run to the bank."

"I see, we'll fix that problem later, for now, let's talk to the robbed merchants and then we'll go after the thieves."

*

The two merchants described the same facts. Five outlaws dressed in standard cowboy clothes, all wore a face bandana, all rode neutral horse colors of sorrels, chestnuts, and bays. All heading southwest to Temple.

After loading with vittles and jungle warfare contraptions, the Trio was off. PF was tracking the fresh tracks the galloping horses were leaving in the road. After an hour of hard riding, the Trio stopped to water and rest the horses. Gail asked, "do you think they will stop in Temple, take a hotel room and hop on a train to Austin in the morning?"

"That's what normal travelers would do, but outlaws think differently. They won't want to be seen in town until it's time to buy tickets. That means, they'll set up an outside camp tonight, and never even think the law would be after them. But we'll be there to give them a reception, for sure!"

After tracking them all day, they finally smelled camp smoke. Finding a spot with good grass they ground tethered their horses. On moccasins, they made their way to within 100 yards of camp. Gail whispered, "what is the plan of attack?" Branch answered, "PF and I designed a method for igniting dynamite from 100 yards. We lay a wire over the campfire and attach a stick of dynamite at the far end of the wire while the other end is tied to a cord that will reach us at 100 yards. At the right time, we pull the cord enough to lay the dynamite in the fire and the rest is catastrophic. Of all the jungle warfare we've tried, this is the method that disables the outlaws and allows us to make arrests without shooting them all dead."

PF adds, "now in this case, we don't know if these thieves are wanted dead or alive, or not even wanted as newbies to the owlhoot trail. Plus, after the explosion, as we run into their camp, you'll see why this is the safest way of arresting violent outlaws."

Meanwhile, in the outlaw camp, the whiskey was going down and the leader started counting the heist. "Well boys, we got $10,000 from those two merchants, but the big surprise was walking in the bank and surprising the bank president standing inside the vault getting ready to open the bank. Although he only had $8,000 in cash, we forced him to admit that two mercantiles, Bowman and Wadsworth, were late in making their deposits. Of course, that's after I broke two of his fingers"—followed by laughs, guffaws and more whiskey.

About two hours past midnight, every outlaw was out snoring and half comatose from the whiskey. After setting the dynamite surprise, Branch then asked PF to go ahead and shoot the coffee pot. The shot rang out with a clang and as the five outlaws jumped up with a gun in hand, Branch pulled the cord some 2-3 feed to place the dynamite in the coals.

The Trio had special ear plugs provided by the railroad dynamite crew. After jumping behind trees or boulders, placing their hands over their ears, the massive explosion went KABOOM. The concussive wave still managed to reach the 100 yards, rustled the Trio's clothing, and even blew their hats off their hands. Gail wondered what devastation would occur in camp.

Running into camp, the horses had scattered, fires were starting all over camp, the outlaws' gear was strewed all over the place, and several outlaws had been either lifted up or just blown over. All the pistols were on the ground safely away from the stumbling outlaws. Some of the outlaws were on their hands and knees, busy upchucking and dry heaving.

It was Branch who yelled, "Ok boys, this is the end of the road. You're all under arrest for robbery and what other crimes you have under your belt." One outlaw bent down to pick up his pistol, as PF threw his war club and crushed the outlaw's hand. With Gail holding her pistol on the gang, Branch and PF quickly manacled each outlaw to their own tree with their hands in their back and around the tree. Even their ankles were manacled.

PF then suggested, "the town is without a lawman. It will take all day to get these five goons to jail. Assuming you can do this trip, then I will return tonight by traveling in the road and I'll be back by noon. What do you say?" "Sounds good to me, we'll see you tomorrow afternoon."

It was too late to get some shuteye after spending an hour to put out all the sentinel fires caused by the explosion of the campfire. So, they restarted a cooking fire and started preparing breakfast. Branch was cooking bacon and Gail was frying potatoes and making coffee.

After breakfast, they gathered the horses, and then started loading the outlaws one by one. For security, they kept their hands manacled behind their backs and one ankle was manacled to one stirrup. After they were all loaded, Branch gave them all a speech. "We're riding straight to Waco. We're not stopping except to rest and water the horses. If nature calls, do it in your pants. We don't care an iota about your needs. If you fall off your horse, then you'll get trampled for all we care. If you mouth off, then you are going to lose some teeth from the butt of my Mare's leg."

The ride back to town was without trouble, probably because all five outlaws were still under the effect of a concussion. Arriving at the sheriff's office, PF came outside to greet them. "We were lucky to arrest them without any killing. I checked the wanted posters and these are the Winn gang out of Austin where they killed three bank patrons on their spree. They all have high bounties."

Gail said, "so, that's why we found almost $27,000 in their saddlebags." "Yes, and judge Hobart will be here tomorrow for the trials. I will notify him of the Winn's gang capture so he can bring witnesses from Austin. He may change his mind and send for a secure prisoner boxcar instead; and bring all these outlaws to Austin." "Well, I hope he includes some deputy marshals, otherwise, the responsibility will fall on us, heh? Now if you don't mind, we need to clean up and get some food."

On their way back to the hotel, Branch suggested he get a change of clothes and get a bath, shave and haircut at the tonsorial shop next door while Gail could bathe in her own bathtub. "If you finish before me, wait for me in the hotel lobby since you'll be done before I add the shave and haircut."

As expected, Gail was done before Branch. After opening her door and turning around to lock her door, she felt a pain in the back of her head, and everything went black.

Branch then walked back to the hotel. Entering the lobby, Gail was nowhere. He walked down the hall and recognized that the air was redolent of her perfume. Their room was not locked, and the key was on the floor. Realism set in and without realizing that he was not talking to anyone in particular added, "oh my God, she has been kidnapped. It is time to put an end to this human trafficking outfit. After I rescue Gail, I will never leave her again. Being hornswoggled once is the fault of the violent nature of this land, the second time will be my fault—never again!"

***

CHAPTER 7

Human Trafficking

Branch took off at a run to see PF at the office. "PF, Gail has been kidnapped." "Oh no, well we may be in luck. Pappy was just over here to say that he had followed Dirty Dick Banks to a warehouse where he believes the hostages are kept before transferring them to College Station. Let's go to his boarding house and talk to him."

Once Pappy was informed of the situation, he said, "we have to rescue her this morning, since there is a transfer to College Station sometime today. We can walk there since it's only a 5-minute walk. We don't want to arrive with horses that would tip our hat." On their way, Pappy added, "this dude is a real psychopath, if he opens the door with a gun in hand, since he knows who you are, you only have a second to shoot him before he shoots you." "Fear not, that animal is dead meat!"

Arriving at the warehouse, the entrance door was without a window. Pappy knocked and waited. "Whose there? "It's me, Pappy. I have some important news about that new marshal in town." "How did you know about this place anyways?" "I followed you days ago. Now, I'm not telling you the news by talking thru the door, open up or I walk!"

After a short time, with Branch placing himself in front of the door, the latch was released, and the door started to open. As soon as Branch saw the outlaw's gun, he fired. In slow motion, Banks face became distorted in shock as his body flexed from the point-blank load of 00 Buckshot hitting him in his mid-section. His body became propelled rearward as his arms and legs trailed behind his body. Hitting the floor, all the hostages screamed as they heard Banks groan twice before he went still.

As the Trio stepped inside, one man had his hands up in surrender as another was holding a pistol to Gail's head. Branch stepped up to the outlaw with his DA pistol in hand. He made it clear as he said, "Mister, if you as so much put your thumb on that hammer to cock it, I will shoot you dead." The outlaw was frozen in thought as Branch saw Gail put her hand in her riding skirt side pocket. In slow motion, Gail pushed her hand down toward her crotch as a gunshot was heard. The outlaw immediately collapsed to the floor with his pistol harmlessly falling out of his hand. The outlaw was caterwauling like a cat in heat as he was trying to grab his foot.

"Gail, how did you manage to shoot him?" "I had my derringer hidden in my underpants. Actually, I was pointing at his crotch, but missed." Suddenly, Branch yells, "Gail your riding pants are on fire!" Gail looks down, yanks her skirt down to her ankles and starts pulling and tearing at her underpants which were also on fire. By the time she stepped clear of the burning clothes, there she stood naked from the waist down. Branch, who wasn't going to waste the moment, added, "that's a mighty nice black furry triangle. You may want to cover yourself before I get distressed, heh?" "For sure. As one of the hostage ladies hands her a slip-in-skirt, she nonchalantly dresses herself. "One day, you'll have to explain how you kept that derringer from falling into your vital private parts." "That's simple, a cloth holster was tied to my Hoosier belt and........." "Never mind, that's too private for now, heh?" "For sure!"

Pappy then took over. "I know where the receiving warehouse is in College Station. But we don't know where the original holding area is in Dallas. Maybe these outlaws can enlighten us." The man with his hands up added, "I don't know a thing, my job is to guard the hostages and bring them water and food. Whitlow on the floor has been in Dallas, so he might know."

"Well, if he knows, he's going to tell us." Branch took the outlaw's boot and yanked it off. The outlaw let out a wail that shook everyone in the room. "Mister, I want the address and names of people in Dallas that are in charge of this trafficking trail." "I can't tell you that, cause if

I do, I'm a dead man." "Well not to beleaguer the point, but assuming you don't die from a foot infection, you're going hang for kidnapping. Now, were you to cooperate with me, I would speak on your behalf during your trial and ask for you to get a prison sentence instead of the rope."

The outlaw wasn't buying, so PF stepped on his shot-up foot as wailing and screaming restarted. "We can do this all day, since you enjoy it so much." Again no response, as Branch grabbed his foot and rotated it about. This time the outlaw passed out. Gail then added, "well that isn't going to work. PF, do you still carry that awl?" "Why of course, it's in a sleeve behind my pistol." "Great, throw some water in his face and let's wake him up for the 'coup de resistance.'"

Branch added, "let me do the honors." Branch straddled the outlaw and pressed his knees onto the outlaw's forearms. As quick as he forced the lower jaw open, he shoved the awl's tip in the crater of a black molar. The result was instantaneous—the eyeballs crossed, the limbs went stiff and spread out, was incontinent of urine, and squealed like a rabbit stuck in a leg trap. When Branch withdrew the awl, the look of horror was frozen on Whitlow's face. "Now that was impressive, are you ready for round two of at least six more teeth ready for the poker."

"Stop, stop, stop. Get that thing away from me. Is that deal still on the table?" "Only with the address and the organizer's name." "The warehouse address is 81 Cornwall Street in the abandoned factory district. The big boss is Worley Sutton, owner of the Lucky Ace of Hearts Casino on South Craymore Street."

After closing up the warehouse and sending Banks to the undertaker, Whitlow was brought to the Doctor's Hospital for surgery on his foot. Afterwards, the four hostages were treated to the use of one hotel room, for four baths and four hot meals at the General Hotel. When Branch went to get six tickets for the next train to Dallas, Gail, with PF as an escort, went to buy four new dresses and accessories for the hostage ladies. The last-minute activity was packing a change of clothes for both Gail and Branch and included fresh panty underwear for Gail. The train left at

3PM and it would take four hours to cover the 100 miles.

Whereas PF and Pappy's train to College Station left at 11AM, and both could return to Waco by midnight with the hostages and guards holding them prisoners. Meanwhile, the Duo went to Bessie's Diner for a private talk and meal. Branch started, "I was lucky today, but I could have lost you." "Is that why you sent PF with me to buy clothes for the ladies?" "I guess so. You see, I promised the Almighty, that if I got you back, that I would never leave you alone ever again."

"Whoa, that is noble but not realistic. Some people are not born to die young. I believe that we are both in that selected group. We are both going to be together till we grow old and senile." "Heck, I'm already a borderline babbling idiot trying to say that I love you so, that it hurts." "Is that a proposal?" "Well, it's the only one you're going to get." "Then, not to miss the moment, I accept. I will marry you, love you, be your friend, business partner and bear your children if we are blessed. I want to be the only person on earth that you can trust 100%." "No man can ask any more, I only hope to prove to you my love, my respect and total financial and emotional support." They then joined hands and leaned over the table for a passionate kiss as the waitress arrived with their steaks. "The cook may have undercooked them, but I see there's enough heat at this table to keep the steaks cooking, for real!"

At 3PM, the six of them boarded the train. Branch gave each lady $100 in paper currency to cover their expenses till their families were located. At 7PM, they arrived at the railroad terminal. Waiting for them was the City Marshal and one deputy. "Hello, US Marshals West and Woods, we knew you were coming because we were notified by District Judge Fields of your arrival and plans to raid the trafficking warehouse. We hope you know where that is, cause we have no idea after looking several months for it. I'm Marshal Newfelt and this is Deputy Stickney." "Not only do we know where the hostages are waylaid, we know the organizer and head boss. With your help, we're putting an end to this plague today." "Lead the way, Marshal!"

Marshal Newfelt had a three-seat buggy waiting and drove off with their luggage. Heading to 81 Cornwall, Branch was told by Marshal Newfelt that these kidnappers would fight and shoot to the end since they all knew they were facing the rope on the gallows. He suggested that we start shooting first and not put our lives in danger. If we get killed, the hostages will automatically be executed as the outlaws make their escape. The marshal emphasized, "it's time to kill or be killed."

Stopping a block away from the address, the lawmen walked the rest of the way. Deputy Stickney was sent to the rear door with instructions to shoot anyone coming out holding a gun. At the door, Branch pointed his shotgun sideways and blew off the lock and door handle. Rushing in was bedlam. There were four outlaws with their guns drawn. When the shooting started, the hostages collapsed to the floor, as the outlaws were put down one after the other. Looking back, each of the lawmen had shot one of the outlaws. After the shooting ceased, there was a shot at the back of the warehouse. When Marshal Newfelt went to investigate, he found his deputy standing over the last of the outlaw guards.

So there it was, five dead outlaws and seven very grateful local gals set free of a nightmarish life in a foreign land. Deputy Stickney was given the job of getting the undertaker, confiscating cash, guns and horses in the rear barn, and taking care of the seven ladies. The Trio then headed to South Craymore Street at the Lucky Ace of Hearts Casino to visit with Worley Sutton.

The Trio entered the establishment and found every gambling game was with standing room only. The master gambling wheel had a man on each of the 36 numbers with a minimum bet of $1 and a maximum bet of $5 per person, per number, and per turn of the wheel. Some gamblers had their $5 on several numbers. With three attendants watching, no one dared to cheat and add a late bet as the master wheel was slowing down. With the heavy drinking, the gamblers tended to be rowdy. The pay was four times the bet, and that meant the house always won.

The remainder of the hall was mixed with poker, blackjack and several tables for Faro. The heavy rollers were standing by the craps table and taking their chance with unlimited betting. The ladies seemed to prefer dice with a lower bet minimum of two bits as their husbands were giving away their ranches. Along with all this was the continuous piano playing of lively ragtime tunes. Unique to this casino, was watered down free drinks if you were gambling.

Gail saw all she wanted to see as Branch asked one of the bouncers where they could find Mister Sutton. When told to go upstairs overlooking the main casino, Branch and Gail took off with the marshal. Arriving at the office, Marshal Newfelt said he would stay outside to prevent bouncers from jumping in the fracas. Plus he said, he didn't want to know how the Duo was going to get Sutton to admit to his deeds.

After talking over a plan, the Duo entered without knocking, Gail immediately spotted Sutton's bodyguard standing next to Sutton's desk. Simultaneously, the Duo attacked. Gail shoved a marlin nail into the bodyguard's right nostril a pushed it till it exited at the top of his nose. At the same time, Branch slammed the butt of his Mare's Leg on the top of Sutton's gun hand, hard enough to break several bones.

Sutton was screaming out in pain while the bodyguard, with bugeyes, was salivating and drooling all over Sutton's desk. Gail added, "if you go for your gun, I'm going to pull this nail with both hands and split your nose in two. Now shut up and act like a man you wimp."

Finally, Sutton spoke up, "I'm going to kill you for this, now what do you want?" "I'm arresting you for kidnapping and human trafficking. The marshal is outside to bring you to jail. But before that, I want you to hand over all the money you made in the past months from feeding ladies to the port in Texas City." "Yeah, right. Over my dead body." "I don't think so, certain pain has a way of loosening someone's tongue. You will be making restitution to the families so help my God, or I will torture you to death right here."

Branch then not too gently manacled Sutton's hands in back of his chair. Out came the awl and it's first application brought a look of terror on Sutton's face followed by kicking and squirming of a dying predator. Sutton's screams were clearly heard all over the gaming tables. Branch then decided to try a different method, to embarrass him in front of his patrons. Out of his bag of 'possibles' came a pair of pliers. Without missing a second, he grabbed his front incisor and pried it out. Sutton wet himself and soiled his pants. The second incisor came out slower to make the pain last longer. With both incisors out, Branch pulled a bull ring and after unsnapping the lock, pushed it thru his nose septum and relocked it in place. Sutton was out of control, cussing and threatening every living soul on earth. Branch was not listening, he opened Sutton's fly, grabbed his manhood and was about to cut it off when Sutton yelled "55-2-19."

Branch then manacled Sutton's ankles, and the bodyguard's ankles and wrists, as Gail pulled out the marlin nail. With Marshal Newfelt present as witness, the safe opened on the first try, and a pile of money was collected. By a quick count, there was +-37,000.

As Marshal Newfelt was walking the prisoners out, he yelled out that the casino was closing. All the game managers were ordered to return the earnings to the players and in no time the place was empty after everyone had seen Sutton with a bull ring in his nose and smelling like a privy.

As they were all walking to the jail, Marshal Newfelt asked Branch how he wanted to divide the money. "Divide the safe money between the families of the lost ladies. Collect the guns and horses and send those funds to Captain Ennis. Keep the pocket cash from the dead outlaws, the bodyguard, and Sutton. Have the town council legally confiscate the casino and sell it at auction. If there are any bounty rewards on anyone, Gail and I will accept those funds. We're staying overnight at the Princess Hotel and will check with you tomorrow before the 3PM train back to Waco."

*

Walking hand in hand some three blocks to their hotel, the Duo was silent. Entering the hotel lobby, Branch paid for a suite with its own water closet/tub. "Let's bring our overnight bags to our room and then we can get something to eat. Entering their room, Gail said, "I am hungry, not for food, but for you. Now that we are engaged, I feel it is time to step up our intimacy." Branch, not knowing how to respond, simply took her in his arms and kissed her passionately. Gail then stepped back, unbuttoned her blouse, dropped her riding skirt and her personal undies. There she stood naked. "Take a good look, this is what you are getting and it's the complete package, not just that furry triangle that you saw by accident."

Branch realized that he was staring, but managed to say, "I fell in love with you not because of your body, but because you are totally gorgeous—body and mind. Was this all meant to be? If so, how one man can be so fortunate is beyond fairness."

Walking up to him, she said, "now it's your turn." Branch proceeded to strip and once his manhood fell out, Gail simply said, "Oh my, how can any woman be so lucky."

"You know, Gail, that I've never been with a woman and so I feel rather shy and awkward, having never had a dalliance." "And as a lifelong tomboy and independent woman, I have never been with a man. Maybe we can learn together." "Yes, but if you agree, could we not consummate our love till after our marriage. Yet, we need to learn how to pleasure ourselves intimately." "Then join me in bed and pander me." "What is pander?" "Indulge yourself and satisfy me, then I will do the same to you."

After several minutes of kissing, roving hands, and touching, Gail said, "I am ready for you, bring me to my nirvana as she guided his hand to her private area. Gail quickly responded and suddenly her eyes rolled backwards, the body arched, and when her contractions started, she lost consciousness. When her contractions peaked for the last time, she awoke. She was silent for a while and finally said, "I went to a peaceful and pleasurable place that is impossible to describe. Will I ever experience that again?" "Relations are like a bell; it will ring again and again for years."

After a passionate kiss, Gail saw that Branch was in full tumescence. She gently touched him, and Branch could not hold back. The inevitable happened as the contractions started and he spilled his seed. Gail was proud to see that he had responded to her touch and added, "Mister West, we're going to keep emptying your reservoir, or I'm going to end up with triplets"— as both broke out in laughter.

After drawing a full tub of hot water, the Duo jumped in together. Although, they each started scrubbing with a bar of scented soap, it quickly progressed to touching. Branch exclaimed, "now that I know your sensual spots, I can't get enough of you." "Well, I'm not a wanton woman, but I know my urges and I enjoy my passions." "Then let's dry off and pleasure ourselves again."

Eventually, the lovers fell asleep. On awakening, after their morning ablutions, another round of loving followed. After getting dressed, they headed downstairs to the hotel restaurant for breakfast. Sitting down at a table, Branch added, "boy that running hot water in the water closet with a sink and toilet is a far advancement over the standard Ewer, basin, and chamber pot. That's going to be the first thing I add to your ranch house, heh?" "You're too late, when two teenage girls hit puberty at the same time and started menstruating, Uncle Otis immediately had a well dug, a windmill pump installed with inside plumbing and a fully stocked water closet with tub and washing machine." "Why the washing machine?" "For women's hygiene, for sure!" After they placed their order of four scrambled eggs, bacon, home-fries, buttered toast with jam and coffee, Branch added, "we have plenty of time to spend before our train, what do you say we discuss another subject on raising horses? "For sure, what do you want to talk about?" "Mares, stallions and foals!"

"Starting with mares. We raise them as breeding stock or riding mounts. Some would easily qualify as racing horses and the wrangler would point those out. Mares come in heat as early as 18 months, but we don't breed them till they are 3 years old. Which is the classic example that there are years of maintaining horses till they mature to an age when they can provide their productive share. Fortunately, we have now reached this crucial level and have horses for sale each year."

"Not to take you off your stride, but can you review the heat signs?" "Sure, mares come in heat every 21 days. They don't bleed, their tails are up, their vulva is swollen, they squat down, they show interest in geldings and stallions, they become aggressive and difficult to handle and ride, as well as being unpredictable. And all this lasts +-3 days throughout March to October."

"From now on, I'll choose my questions carefully, and one day you'll have to tell me what 'vulva' means, heh?" "For sure."

"Breeding is done by two methods. The natural method is to release a stallion and a mare in heat in their own paddock. They will mate twice a day for the heat's duration. The insemination rate is consequently very high.

The other method is the assisted type. We bring a mare into the stallion's stall and let them breed daily for three days as we separate them between mating sessions. This also provides a high insemination rate but is more dangerous for the handlers."

"The mare's gestation is +-11 months. Even today, it is not well understood why birthing, also called foaling, occurs at night. Foaling occurs in the pasture or in a foaling stall. It occurs within 5 minutes and very few mares, unless it's their first foaling, need assistance. Usually, we find the foal all cleaned up by morning and already nursing. The placenta has been eaten by the mare to prevent attracting predators. The ingested placenta helps provide the hormones to close up the uterus. Last of all, we try to rebreed the mares on their first cycle after foaling, because we try to maintain a yearly foaling as close as possible. In closing, mares tend to reproduce till age +- 15 years."

They interrupted their discussion when their meals arrived. Finishing eating, with a fresh pot of coffee at hand, Gail started again. "Foals are the pride of any horse ranch. Their birth coat is not definitive till they lose their baby hair. Our ratio generally runs 60% colts and 40% fillies. Generally, the foals survive on mother's milk for the first month."

"Most ranchers don't realize that unlike cattle with their large udder and four teats, horses are like humans, with two udders and two teats." "Really, you had to add that like you added vulva and mating twice a day, heh?" "For sure"—with a smile from ear to ear.

Continuing, "foals nurse till four months or sooner if the mare becomes pregnant. Fortunately, most foals eat hay and grain by 3 weeks of age. The nutritional need for foals is 1 pound of hay and 1 pound of weaning grain per month of age per day. Even if the foals are weaned off the teat, they tend to stay with their mother till at least 9 months of age."

"Now moving on, let's talk about geldings. They are the basis of horse ranching. Every gelding will end up in one of three functions— field work horses, harnessed mounts on wagons, and the basic riding mount. Geldings have a calmer disposition that makes them trainable and workable. The best time to geld them is under one year of age to avoid puberty. Early gelding allows bone growth plates to stay open leading to taller and bigger adults. Doc Harris does our geldings, and we get less 'proud cuts.'" "Now, you know I'm going to ask you what that means?" "A 'proud cut' is a partial gelding done by inexperienced wranglers. They have the testicles removed but residual reproductive tissue remains that allows them to produce some sperm—if you want to know more, talk to Doc Harris."

"There are two other conditions that occur in geldings. The first is a 'rig.' A hidden third testicle in the horse's belly which produces altered sperm that leads to low quality foals. The last is info that most people don't realize, one third of properly gelded horses still get an erection, can mate, ejaculate, but without sperm."

"Moving on to stallions, they are a dangerous animal that is aggressive, unpredictable and not trustworthy. We only allow the two trainers and our wrangler to handle and care for them. We do raise some for sale to ranchers who want to breed their own stock. We start breeding them at age 3, but if necessary, we start them as early as 2 years old. As you might suspect, we keep three color coats to match our mares—sorrel, chestnut and bay. We pasture our stallions with the geldings since they do not do well if kept in a stall waiting for breeding. Now the one issue always brought up is when to retire a stallion. As long as a stallion is healthy, manageable, can set a mare, inseminate them, and produce quality foals, we keep them active."

"You are simply unbelievable. I realize you have spent a lifetime learning all this, but still, you really know your animals. We talked about the type of horse you raise, the ranch itself, feeding horses, and now the different horse sexes. I really want to see your operation. What do you say we head back home and spend a few days off so we can visit your ranch." "No dear, we can visit OUR ranch, hey?"

*

With five hours on their hands before they boarded the train, Branch asked the hotel clerk if he knew of any horse races nearby. The clerk answered, "we have Quarter horse races every day starting at 11AM at the McGalloway Racetrack. After taking a taxi ride to the race grounds, the Duo stood by the finishing line of the standard quarter mile. Branch bought a stopwatch from a local vendor and then picked a conversation with an older gentleman standing next to them.

"What is special about the racetrack ground?" "Nothing but the standard reddish Texas dirt with red clay and high in iron. The difference is the fresh back blading between each racing block." At the sound of a starting gun shot, Branch pressed his stopwatch to start. The winner was a young filly at 22 seconds. The second race had a stallion at 19 seconds. The third race was another stallion at 20 seconds. The last race of this block was the well-advertised older stallion known to occasionally break 18 seconds at eight years of age. Gail was clearly excited at the thrill of viewing the short time to the finish line. The last race started, and the horse never disappointed anyone by coming in at 17 seconds. Branch only noticed the size, shape, musculature, and general disposition of this magnificent animal.

Gail asked the nearby gentleman what this last horse was worth. "This horse has two qualities that establishes his worth. He is wanted for breeding with a high stud fee. He is also a racing contender. I bet his current value is in the range of $10,000." "Well thank you for your info, we are Branch West and Gail Woods soon to be wed." "That is wonderful, and I'm Wilbur McGalloway, owner of this racetrack and that winning old stallion." "Well sir, nice to meet you. I suspect we'll meet again since we're going to start adding racing horses to our horse ranch—the Circle W, in Waco."

"Whoa, I know that brand. I have seen several Quarter horses with that brand win many races in the past years. You had better get your workers to start pulling out the fittest of horses and start training them. I'm sure you'll find some winners." Gail answered, "I'm certain that my fiancé is already planning to do so. We'll see you again, for sure! By the way, what are your winnings on that last race with the older stallion?" "A mere $2,000 and a lot of pride. Good day Ma'am."

*

On their way to Waco, Gail couldn't stop talking about the thrill of watching the races. "Do we have races in Waco and if not, where are the nearest races?" "Well we know they have them in Dallas, and I suspect there will be some in Austin as well. Both of these cities are 100 miles or 3-4 hours away on train. Plus Temple and Georgetown on the way to Austin may have some as well. But for now, we need to get a team of racers into a training mode." "I'm sure that our wrangler and trainers can choose some candidates and you can always wire your money to Anson Aiken in Pueblo and get those horses here." "Ok, but for now, we have a 3-4-hour ride ahead and let's talk some more about our horses and ranch."

"Fine, what's the subject matter today?" "It's a group of short questions. The first, when you and Otis say we have +-200 horses, how do they spread in ages and types?" "First of all, we have more horses than mentioned. We have 173 Quarter horses. Broken down, 50 are mares in reproductive age, 50 are foals to age one. 35 are 2-years old, and 35 are 3-years old. Although we tend to sell our horses at age 3, we often sell 2-years old for riding and light harness work with personal buggies. Plus we keep three stallions of the three coats. Now the Belgians total 80. We keep 20 mares for reproduction, 20 are foals to age one. 20 are 2-years old, 10 are 3-years old and 10 are 4-years old, plus two stallions. So 173 and 82 equals 255 to be exact."

"This second question is to satisfy my curiosity. What commands are the horses taught before their sale?" Verbal commands for riding horses include: walk, whoa, stand and wait, gee(R), haw(L), and back up. For harness work they are the same as riding, plus over(step aside), pick up foot, go away(when crowding handler or team horse). Just as important is the tactile touch of spurs or foot as pressure is applied or released. And the one command that is used for bad behavior is 'aaah.' Besides these, we know the new owner will add his own personal ones."

"Well done. Now a bit of discussion on selective breeding." "Uncle Otis started documenting the result of mixing the sorrel stallion with the three-color coat mares, and repeating the same with the other two stallions. We now know the result of each mating. Meaning the genetic makeup and physical qualities of each foal is determined within a few months of age. As some Quarter horse examples, a smooth walker will be a rider, a small agile foal will end up a cow horse and the good size colts will end up being gelded. The Belgians are easier, they all end up as work horses unless a mare is kept for breeding. Now racing will be a new area where selection of breeding stock will have some guessing and common-sense planning involved for some time."

"Yes, I can see that your present system is well proven, and I'll be on the ground-work for building a racing division. Now talk to me a bit about the three functional categories of horses you presently select for and raise for sale."

"Ok, the three groups are harness/work horses, cow horses, and riding stock. The work horses have to be trained as a single horse vs a team of two horses. Trainability with a harness is absolutely necessary. These can be mares or geldings. These horses, +-16 hands, have to be responsive to commands. Each sub-category is specifically trained; light duty on a buggy and buckboard, medium duty on large wagons, harrows and light farm implements, and heavy-duty draft horses, +-17 hands, on freight wagons and double-bladed plows. And to this end the large gelding fits all these categories except the freight wagon and double edge plow. That is why, this horse is our number one seller."

"The cow horse is always in demand. Any of our small foals are placed in this category. The 3-yearolds, usually +-15 hands or less, are also mares or geldings. These horses are quick and agile. They must be trainable to be rein and foot responsive, able to cut cattle, and good at rope and hold techniques. We keep 100 head of cattle not only for beef, but as training animals."

"Now the third class is the riding horse. These are grouped in three categories depending on the weight of the rider: <120 lbs. = 14 hands, 120— 180 lbs. = 15 hands, and >180 lbs. = 16 hands. Again these can be mares or geldings. Some of these horses are short distance mounts whereas some are more durable and are long distance riders. The quality of the ride determines the higher value. A gentle nature is required to facilitate bonding with the owner. Some of these horses need to be ridden every day and don't do well left in a livery or barn stall all day. So, we guarantee that these horses all come as a response to a whistle, which allows them to be kept in a pasture more than in the barn. The final test of readiness, the horse must be saddle friendly and accept a saddle and rider without rearing, bucking or biting."

"Ok, next, what is the functional difference between a trainer and a horse whisperer?" "A whisperer is a patient and easy-going horseman. They are used to solve a horse's bad traits. By using gentle methods and taking advantage of a horse's innate sense, together they resolve bad traits without using violent methods such as beating or bronc busting. To simplify, they get horses settled down and ready for trainers. A true fact, the whisperer saves many a horse from the meat or glue factory. To bust a common myth, whisperers do not whisper magic words in horses' ears!"

"Now trainers have either experience or schooling in horsemanship. They have the responsibility of preparing a young horse for its designated function. Again, trainers have to be gentle but firm in their directions. It can be a long process, but buyers want a horse ready for its function. That is why planting crops is so important in training work horses. We guarantee all our sales with a replacement or a 100% refund."

"Nice job, my last question is regarding finances. Otis said that the business can generate a $1,500 profit with absolutely all expenses covered. Can you break down these into expenses and income?" "I can do better. At the deed transfer, Otis handed me a summary sheet of last year's income and expenses. Here it is:

INCOME

Sale of surplus hay.................$2,000
Harnesses...........................$3,000
Sale of 60 horses @$150.........$9,000
Stud fees...........................$1,000

Total income....$15,000

EXPENSES

Vet....................................$250
Feed grain..........................$250
Harness supplies....................$500
Blacksmith/farrier supplies.......$250
Food.................................$1,000
Seed..................................$200
Chicken feed........................$150
Coal and firewood...................$300
Ammunition..........................$300
Personals............................$300
Seasonal harvest workers...........$500
Labor—full timers..................$6,500

Petty cash............................$500

Total expenses...........$11,000

BUSINESS PROFIT.....$4,000

BALANCE

Minimum bank account...........$1,000

Replacement AG equipment....$1,000 (now up to $3,000)

Building upgrades................$500 (now up to $1,500)

Absolute business profit....$1,500 To Savings Acct."

"Wow, I am amazed and pleased. You have a going concern and a profitable business to fall back on." "Now tell me how you want to change things." "The normal operations of raising the horses must not be changed unless we add another 50-100 horses. That will be your decision. I am interested in adding 100 more acres of hay for sale. To pay for your increasing the herd and a higher profit margin. The racing horse division will be separate of the horse ranch, and never affect the survival of the ranch. As we are approaching home, assuming we are going to the ranch tonight, here is an agenda I would like to discuss with the workers in the morning and then the interview with the foreman. Do you agree with each item since you're going to be at my side to answer questions?"

Gail read each agenda, smiled and said, "Agree 100% and I think we should start the meeting by inviting all the workers to a paid day at our wedding, heh?" "For sure."

*

Stepping off the train, PF was waiting for them with a look of alarm on his face. "What's wrong PF?" "Judge Hobart arrived last night and was kidnapped by outlaws this morning. They want some of their buddies released in exchange for the judge. They are holed up in the Rusty Bucket saloon and there are five of them—all gunfighters."

"Well, we cannot allow outlaws to threaten our judges and we don't negotiate with outlaws. Guess we are heading for a gunfight. The Trio headed over and Branch looked over the batwing doors to assess the situation. To his shocking surprise, Judge Hobart was standing on a wooden box with a noose around his neck tied to a ceiling beam and his hands were tied behind his back. The only other person in the saloon, other than the outlaws, was the barkeep.

The Trio stepped aside, and Branch presented the situation. "It appears that there will be five gunfighters separated as wide as they can. Gail, you take down the outlaw on the judge's right as PF you take the one to his left. I will go after the other three which will be widely spaced. If any of the outlaws kick off the wooden box, I hope either of you can cut that rope down with a bullet, or the judge won't be able to talk for a week nor turn his neck for a month."

Stepping inside, the outlaw speaker started. "So you're the new US Marshal. Well, let me tell you how this will play out. Either we get the two Ganter brothers in the next hour or else we'll hang the judge and fight our way out. We'll pick them up on our way out of town. Which will mean that the three of you will be dead."

Branch then responded. "No, this is not going to play out your way. You are all under arrest, put your hands up or get ready to draw. None of you are making it out alive." The outlaws responded in their true altruistic way by kicking away the box under the judge's feet and pulling their pistols. In that instant the Trio responded with gun fire. There were three shotgun blasts and two pistol shots followed by the rope twang made by Gail's lead bullet as the judge landed on his butt.

PF took the noose off the judge's neck and helped him stand as he cut his wrist bindings. "Well, you must be Miss Woods, and thank you for your superb accuracy. Now I am glad to meet the two of you, Marshal West and Deputy PF Silver, I presume!"

After small talk and dragging the dead outlaws outside in the street, Judge Hobart presented his plans. "Tomorrow, I will review all the lawmen's statements on each arrest. Then I will confer with the prosecutor and plan for several trials the next day. I have brought with me the necessary witnesses to convict all these outlaws. I am also aware that some of these outlaws assisted the lawmen, and I will take this into consideration at the sentencing of the guilty ones."

"Are you going to need a security detail?" "No, after my disappearance, my court clerk notified the army at the nearby fort and I will be getting a military detail to act as security till the executions. Thanks for the offer, but looking at these killer outlaws, I'd say you did your share."

"Then if it flies with PF, Gail and I are taking a few personal days off to get familiarized with our horse ranch."

***

BOOK TWO
The Circle W Ranch

CHAPTER 8

Learning the Ropes

After picking up their horses, the Duo traveled the road to the ranch. Arriving at 10PM, there was a light in the dining shack. Stepping down, Gail saw the cook and wrangler and ran into their arms. "Gosh, guys, I haven't seen you for a year, I'm so happy to see you're still working here. Oh excuse me, gentlemen, this is Marshal Branch West, my fiancé and co-owner of this ranch. Branch this is our wrangler Zeke Freeman and our cookie Zeb Pike. After some small talk, Zeke took care of the horses and would saddle them at predawn so Gail and Branch could go on an early ride. Zeb then said, "within a half hour I'll bring in some reheated beef stew, fresh bread, butter, apple strudel and coffee."

The Duo stepped inside the ranch house and Branch was impressed. Gail opened some lamps and gave him the tour. A large kitchen with hot and cold water, a cooking stove with oven, a table and a separate scullery with plumbing and a manual clothes washer and wringer. A separate conference type dining room and table. A large parlor and a private office with a separate entrance to the outside porch. The complete water closet was next to the office. The last four rooms were bedrooms. One door had a note tacked to it that explained the new dressers, bed, end tables and rocking chairs— and a new door to the adjoining bedroom. Gail was somewhat confused as she said, "when my parents and my aunt were alive, these were two standard bedrooms." Branch said, "it appears there has been some recent renovations. Otis wanted us to have our new private quarters with access to the nursery, heh?" "It appears that way, for sure!" The other two rooms were Gail's and her sister's room.

As the cookie arrived with a late supper, the Duo sat down and enjoyed their meal. Afterwards, they sat on the parlor sofa. It didn't take much time to find themselves in each other's arms and with mutual pandering, they reached their peak passion together. After the glowing period, Branch said, I love you so much that before I get involved with this ranch, I want to know when we are getting married." "Tomorrow at the District Court would be soon enough for me, but a wedding is not just for the newlyweds. It's for the community, family, friends and workers. Now all those are here in town for my guests. Who are you inviting?" My parents, two brothers and families and every lawman from Durango, to Waco during my bounty hunting days, plus my old boss in Denver." "So my guests are local, except for my sister and a college friend and yours are very distant. Sounds like we need 7-10 days' notice to pull this off. Plus set up the minister, a wedding reception/supper, invitations, a wedding dress and dress suit, rings and possibly other issues I forget such as a honeymoon and more."

"Gosh, all that 'to do' just to make you my wife?" "Yeah, but look at what you're getting?" "Oh I know, I will always have that picture in my head, when I first saw you naked." Somewhat kidding, "is that what I am, a fresh piece of meat?" "To me, you're always going to be hot, but with a brain and a heart. So, are you willing to make the announcement tomorrow to our workers?" "Oh, yeah. Now let's try our new private bedroom."

Despite only a few hours of sleep, the Duo was up before dawn. Walking to the cook shack, Zeb was already at work and handed each a cup of coffee. After they saddled up for their pre-breakfast ride, Gail started, "the ranch is three sections, or 1,920 acres, or three-square miles. The north border starts right here at the ranch house. Behind the house are the pastures and paddocks that extend a full mile south. There is a common access road to the barn for all pastures and they are all fenced in. Riding beyond the mile of pastures and paddocks, they finally arrive at the crop lands. Branch estimated that each parcel was 2,000 ft. long by a depth equal to just below 50 acres. Consistent with his calculations, three of these parcels were noted, side by side, as hay fields. The last section was 50 acres used for oats. To the Duo's surprise, there had been some plowing and harrowing on a new nearly completed 50-acre parcel—to be discussed with foreman Ashburn. Riding back to the ranch, Branch asked what the water supply was for the horses and for irrigating the crops. "We are so fortunate, there is a medium size river that runs the entire east-west direction in the property. There is plenty of water for the horses and for irrigation of our crops if necessary." Branch's last comments as they returned to the ranch was, "I'm amazed that your parents and Otis were able to get three sections that all bordered a main road for three miles long by a mile deep its entire length."

Arriving at the ranch, the workers were having breakfast, so the Duo joined in at Zeb's insistence. When it got to coffee, Gail got up and pounded a spoon on her empty plate. "It's nice to see you after a year and I have several announcements. First, I'm back and here to say,

I have a new partner, Marshal Branch West, and you're all invited to our wedding in 10 days. Whistles, hoots and hollers followed. Branch is smart, kind and a good man. He will make a great boss and it is the man I fell in love with. You have always been respectful of my family, and I hope you will soon include Branch. Comments—fair enough, fair enough with applause. Here is Branch with a few comments."

"The automobile and tractor are coming to replace the horse. If we are lucky, we have about 15 years before this happens. This gives us some good years to prosper and benefit from the investment made by the Woods' elders. We are not going to change whatever routine you now have. A winning enterprise must be maintained. We do however hope to increase the number of horses to 350. Not to worry, your workload will not increase, we'll get you more help. We will put a bit more emphasis on Belgians since the size of agricultural equipment is getting bigger by the year."

"To accomplish this, we'll build a second barn and increase the bunkhouse to 18 bunks with a sitting/card playing area. To add some amenities, we'll bring hot and cold plumbing with a water closet and shower to your bunkhouse." More hoots and guffaws.

"The one new thing that will affect you is the fact that we will be adding horse racing, as a way of keeping step with the future. More on that will follow. The other new development is that we will be going commercial with planting crops for sale. That will mean a second hay barn, a second bunkhouse, more implements, and a new drive thru implement shed. To reassure, this will be a separate entity and will not affect your work except during harvests when extra help will be needed."

"Ok Gail, would you add the closing plans." "This morning, we will meet with Gary and Annette, check out the barn, hay shed, and bunkhouse. After the noon dinner, we'll meet with Zeb, Zeke and Obadiah. Tomorrow we'll meet with Ansel, Benny, Barney and Buck. After we get back to town, we'll make arrangements with Paul Hall regarding the construction of new buildings. Now keep in mind what these individual meetings are for. We need to know if you're satisfied, if you have problems to discuss, if you want changes made to improve the ranch's bottom line, and we'll reevaluate your salary for next year. That's it." Applause followed as each worker went about his business except for Gary and Annette.

After some small talk, Gail started, "Gary, what is your salary and what benefits do you get." "I make $90 a month with the use of Otis' house on the homestead, plus we get free firewood and coal. Annette and I eat at the cookie shack when we are working. We also get unlimited eggs and fresh garden vegetables. And we get Sunday's off."

Branch said, "that's a start, now what do you do Annette, and what is your salary?" After I drop the kids to school and do some housework, I get here at 9AM and help Zeb with the breakfast dishes and then I do prep work for dinner and supper, clean up the dishes after dinner, feed the chickens, collect the eggs, and weed that garden behind your ranch house. I leave work at 3PM to pick up the kids at school and prepare supper at home for the daily family supper." "And what is your salary?" "Uhh, Annette doesn't get a monetary salary. She gets our benefits just mentioned and occasionally gets the cookie's leftovers which help with our family suppers." "No, no, no," exclaimed Gail. Our workers all get wages and benefits. From now on, I'll be doing the payroll and Annette, since you work 6 hours a day, your pay will be $30 a month plus maintain the same benefits you are now getting."

"Now let's talk about crops. We want to expand our hay to 200 acres and our oats to 100 acres. We want to sell as much hay and straw as possible, and not have to buy oats grain. Can you do this for us?" "Yes sir and look forward to the challenge." "Good, what do you need to make this happen." "Right now, I've hired day workers to start cultivating new land at Otis' order before he left, saying you would want this started early. What I need is 6 full time cropboys like the horse ranch, we'll need several seasonal workers during the harvest. We need a separate bunkhouse, another hay shed

212 Richard M Beloin MD

with a concrete floor, a pull thru equipment shed, a second mower, side rake, hay loader and wagons and another baler. And basic parts for these machines. We don't need more cultivating implements, but we do need the new extra-large manure spreader so we can exchange hay for old manure piles from our neighbors. Lastly, it is time we get a phosphate fertilizer spreader, and start buying phosphate to apply between crops."

"This being winter, what are you doing this time of year?" "We have four Belgian teams working from dawn to dusk, over two worker shifts, doing new ground plowing. We also have four gelding teams doing the harrowing. On the maintenance side we are hauling horse manure to fertilize the hay and oats parcels before spring growth and fertilizing the new cultivated lands before seeding."

"Are you willing to do the hiring of cropboys by yourself?" "Of course, in this case the six temps I now have are great workers and will be happy to go full time. What do I offer them for wages and benefits?" Gail suggests, "for six months, $45 a month with Sunday off, room and board and free pasture for their personal horses. If the worker is worth his salt at six months, then increase it to $60 and found." "Perfect."

Branch adds, "now I know what you'll be doing with the crop side of the business, but what do you do on the horse raising and training side." "It is clear that I'll have to split myself 50/50 from now on. Normally, on a daily basis, I plan the activities of every worker. Not only do I supervise them, but I frequently help them as well. The key is to choose the job that needs my help the most to keep the system working. Since adding a crop entity, I'll have to back off on the helping part, and that will decide who will need a new helper once I'm not available."

"Fair enough, I like that plan. It's called filling a need in a timely fashion. Now in the past year with Gail gone and Otis slowing down, who saw to it to do the selling?" "Simple, when the trainers told me they had, for example, a team of heavy-duty work geldings ready, I would send the same telegram to all my buyers with a firm price, and wait for the positive response, before inviting the buyer to come and check out his purchase."

With the interview done, the Duo decided to visit the bunkhouse, hay shed and barn before dinner. The bunkhouse presently housed 7 workers, and each occupied the bottom bunk for sleeping and the top bunk for their junk. Branch made a note to change things to 16 double bunks, but the top bunks would be converted to a locked cabinet for their junk, and a tall closet would be added at the foot of each bunk for long coats and rifles. Truly a common area, next to the entrance door, was needed with chairs and tables for R&R. Gail added, "yep, it's time to get rid of the shower and a water closet. Men are like pigs, if given the opportunity to stay clean, they will. If not, they will stink and accept it as the norm."

The barn was an amazing structure. Thirty regular stalls, 10 double stalls for foals with their mares, plus 15 extra-large ones for draft horses. It included two foaling rooms and four special stalls for foals with their moms till able to use the double stalls. There was a tact room and a tool room. Upstairs was general storage. Gail added, "this has been functional for the past 15 years, but if changes are needed, we'll find out from Zeke later today." The hay shed allowed a drive thru in the center that allowed unloading to each end. There was a connecting passageway with a concrete floor that acted as a fire brake. There was a big sign in the shed that read 'no smoking or oil lamps allowed.' Branch looked puzzled and finally added, "these two buildings are a big investment of horse lives and a cash crop. Remind me to have the carpenters add a fire wall and a spicket in the connecting passageway."

The noon dinner was a hot meatloaf sandwich with boiled potatoes and coffee. The Duo remarked how good the food tasted. After cleaning up, they met with Zeb. "As cook, is there something you want?" "Not really, we have 75 chickens that I rotate the older non layers each year, and we keep 100 head of cattle for training and supplying our meat. We only butcher steers, old barren cows and injured animals, and we take three every month. We bring the two sides to a butcher shop with a refrigeration cooler. When we need beef, we get what we need, and he charges us 15% of the retail rate to pay for cutting and refrigeration. Our garden produces all the vegetables we need. I have the proper cooking stoves and I have a great helper with Annette." "So you are all set for now, but what happens when we add six ranch workers and a half dozen crop workers? "Then. I will need a fulltime apprentice along with Annette, a larger garden and an extra 25 layers." "Are you satisfied with your wages?" "Yes, I get $60 a month and although I could use another $10, I'm not asking, mind you." "Well, with the more faces to feed, I'm sure we can give you that $10."

The visit with Zeke was a different matter. He was glad to add a second barn and gave the Duo the specific layout. For fire safety, both the new barn and hay shed would be 50 yards away from existing buildings. Zeke made it clear, that he was now at the limit of his physical abilities at age 50. After reviewing all the things he did, it was clear that he had no rest moments from dawn to supper time, seven days a week, including late care provided to ailing horses. Gail finally said, "as soon as the barn goes up, start looking for a young apprentice you can train and work with." "Anything else?" "Yeah, get the blacksmith/ farrier out of the barn to make more room for horses and less of a fire hazard. If you can do that for me, leave my wages the same at $70 a month. I like my work, and like working with these agreeable fellas."

Meeting with the whisperer, Obadiah Clive, was a revelation of personal contentment. "I'm a 60-year-old man, who is perfectly happy to live and work on this ranch. Working with our two trainers is a dream for any whisperers. I think I can continue my work once you add more horses, but if I get behind, you'll be the first to know. At $60 a month, I'm Ok."

With time to spare before supper, the Duo decided to meet with the two trainers, Ansel and Benny. They both admitted that they couldn't take on any more horses to train without some more help and even suggested one full time assistant and a separate trainer to handle race-horses. Benny added, "at $75 a month, we're not asking for more money, just more help." Ansel surprised the Duo when he asked if their wives could find work on the ranch. Gail said, "we need to find a fulltime helper for Zeb, and with so many horses that need to be exercised, we will need an exercising rider. If your wives are interested, have them see Gary."

Supper was a real surprise, canned salmon from Canada was used to make salmon pea wiggle to include hard-boiled eggs and peas in a milk gravy over soda crackers. For some strange reason, it was one of the staff's favorite different meal. To finish the meal, it was apple pie with cheese. After supper, Branch asked where the milk came from since he had not seen a milch cow around the ranch. Gail answered, "well you see, when we hired Zeb he made it clear that this was not a dairy farm and he would not be the one to milk that animal twice a day. "In return for hay, the dairy down the road delivers two gallons each day which Zeb uses for cooking deserts, milk gravy, batter for pancakes, cooking bread and many other cooking uses too many to mention. He never accumulates any surplus since most workers like it in their coffee, or drink it. I strongly recommend that we not try to change this, or the cook will go on strike, heh?" "Well, it certainly sounds like it's a subject worth leaving alone."

After supper, the Duo stayed to visit a while with the men. When they retired to the ranch house, with a pot of coffee, the workers broke out the cards and started playing penny poker in the dining room. Talking in their parlor, they laid out some plans for tomorrow. After meeting with Buck McKenzie, the smithy/farrier, and Barney Bumstead, the harness maker, they agreed to head back to town and check in with PF. If things were quiet, they would conduct some business visits with P. Hall Construction as well as Whitmore's Hardware and Burton's Feed and Seed to order some hay/oats seeds and more agricultural implements.

Barney Bumstead was a young man who branched out from his family's harness business. He went thru his well-equipped shop and showed the Duo his sewing machine, cutting press, rivet setting punch and press, and several hand tools too many to describe. He had a separate room for the leather hides he used to make the harnesses. Of interest were the many pieces of hardware used in connecting the different parts of a harness. Barney then described what he did.

"The horse is left in my shop's lean-to and I fit each piece to the horse's body. I have a leather grade for every degree of work duty. The other thing I do, is make adjustments since some of these horses grow out of their harness before they are sold. I have to admit, that when I have spare time, I do private work for nearby ranches. The cash income is given to Gary for a bank deposit." "So, how come you have your own building?" "Because the horses cannot stand the smell of freshly tinted leather and that's also why I use a lean-to to hold the horses for a fitting."

Branch adds, "seems to me you're pretty well situated. Do you need anything?" "No sir, and I'm perfectly satisfied with my $70 a month because of the excellent room and board—Zeb's cooking is the best."

Arriving at the blacksmith shop situated in the barn, the smithy was heating some bar stock and pounding it into a horseshoe. After making a set pair, he cooled down the forge to meet with the bosses. Gail started, "well Buck, Zeke wants you out of his barn, how do you feel about that?" "The sooner the better, the bar stock is getting harder and I have to run the forge hotter. I'm afraid the chimney may not be insulated enough and so Zeke puts all the horses to pasture when I start the forge." "Then in that case, stop using the forge, start packing, and withing a week you'll have your own shop as soon as we see Paul Hall in town."

Buck didn't believe his ears, "really, that easy?" "Whenever it's for the good of the horses, the answer is yes. Now what else do you need?" "Nothing, not a darn thing as long as you're satisfied with my work. I'm paid $70 a month with fine room and board, and the best group of men to work with." "Are you going to need a helper?" "No sir." "Then make sure you tell the carpenters what you want for a building/lean-to, and keep it at least 75-100 yards from the barns and hay sheds."

The Duo had a hot roast beef sandwich before leaving. As they were saddling their horses, they heard a horse arriving at an all-out gallop. Branch looked up and saw a kid pushing his horse to the max. "Whoa, where you going at that speed, aren't you afraid to ride like that?" "No sir, I love it. My pa is the telegrapher, and I'm allowed to push his horse if the telegram or personal message is within a mile." "What's your name, son?" "Randy Martin." "How old are you?" "Turning 15, real soon." "How would you like to work for this ranch nights and weekends?" "Doing what?" "Racing horses on a quarter mile track." "Why yeah, but you'll have to ask my pa first." "I will, and we'll talk again, heh?"

Gail had already read the personal note, "PF says things are quiet after the executions, but he will need us by tomorrow morning." Arriving in town, PF said, "the trials are now finished and the outlaws who helped us or later turned state's evidence were all given prison sentences in Huntsville. The others were all hung this morning. Things were quiet till Doc Ross came to see me in regard to the beating of a patient with a ruptured spleen. I checked and found the lady had been badly beaten by her husband who is now out of town on business—you know, one of our uppity and arrogant lawyers." "I see, we'll be back as soon as he returns to town. After we run some errands, we'll go to the hospital to talk to that lady and see if she wants to press charges."

Their first stop was the Paul Hall Construction. "Well hello, Gail. What brings you here" "We need a blacksmith/farrier shop with a lean-to, plumbing to the bunkhouse with a water closet and shower, a 50-horse barn with loft, a hay shed to hold 200 tons of hay/straw, a 12 pull-thru shed for agricultural implements, and a second bunkhouse with running water, a water closet, and a shower." "Mercy, that's going to run you about $5,000!" "Oh, I forgot, this is Marshal West, my fiancé and business partner," as Branch smiles and hands Paul a bank voucher for $5,000 as a deposit.

Paul was standing there totally dumfounded while holding the bank voucher. Finally, he said, "well, shall we start laying out some floor plans? I presume you want this all done by tomorrow?" "No, but ASAP and we want to start tomorrow with the blacksmith shop." After two hours of making diagrams, laying out building sizes and agreeing on materials, the Duo left with a contract in hand and a smile on their faces.

At Burton Seed, after introducing Branch to the owner. they ordered timothy, tall fescue, and brome seeds to plant the extra 100 hay acres and enough oat seeds to cover the 50-75 acres. The next stop was the Whitmore Hardware store. Again, after introducing Branch to Roger Whitmore, Gail handed him Gary's list of the agricultural implements they wanted to order. With a $2,000 deposit, the order went in.

On their way to the City Hospital, as the Duo passed by the telegraph office, Branch pulled Gail inside. Joshua Martin greeted them and after some small talk, Joshua said, "and what brings you here today?" Branch took over, "I want to hire your son to work on our horse ranch." "Doing what?" "To be our resident jockey racing our horses." "What, he's just a boy!" "That's true, but I suspect he weighs less than 60 pounds, is small in stature, is skinny as a rail, rides like a pro, and has no fear." "I see!"

"You should see what he can do with your barn horse when he delivers a telegram." "Yeah, I suspected something when old Brownie would be all lathered up after a short trip. What are you offering for pay and what hours?" "One hour every day after school before supper and six hours on Saturday. For $3 a week. When he is my jockey at a local group race, for placing 2nd or 3rd place, he gets $50. If he wins any race, he gets $100. If he gets hurt, we pay all his medical expenses. Like all our employees, he gets a $1,000 life insurance policy." "Way more than fair, let me talk to his mother and we'll get back to you."

Finally arriving at the City Hospital, they quickly got an interview with Doc Ross. "Nice to finally meet you marshal, and hello Gail. I hear there is a wedding in the near future." Gail, smiled and said, "so what is the story about a woman being beaten?" "Rebecca Smorley was brought in the emergency ward, nearly dead. I had to perform an emergency splenectomy. She was full of bruises and had several healed broken bones. She is now recovering, but wants out of her marriage. Unfortunately, three separate court messengers were severely beaten by her husband and we need someone to deliver the court ordered divorce settlements. So, it's either you two, or Mrs. Smorley is doomed." "May we see her and get the papers?" "Certainly, follow me."

Rebecca was sitting by the window and visiting with another lady. After introductions were made, the patient introduced the other lady as her sister who was there to bring her home in Temple. Gail took over, "do you want us to just deliver the divorce papers, or if you are willing to press charges, we'll arrest him and throw him in jail till he pays the divorce settlement." "Yes, here is my signature on the charges, if we don't do it this way, he'll never pay, and I'll have nothing after 10 years of servitude and sexual abuse."

Walking downtown, Branch said, "while you stepped to the water closet, I asked Doc Ross how he beat up those court messengers. Apparently, he has a sap in his right back pocket. So, you're going to have to disable his right hand before you convince him to do what is right." "So you're giving me the lead, heh?" "Yes Ma'am."

Stepping in Smorley's waiting room, the attorney was busy at his desk. Gail stepped in and picked up a heavy glass ashtray off the desk and smashed it as hard as she could on Smorley's hand. Bones and blood were flying everywhere. Smorley grabbed his hand and yelled "Aaarh" you ruined my writing hand, you bitch." I am not a bitch, I'm a pissed off woman who's going to make you release your wife and give her a financial settlement." "Never!"

"Really, let me convince you otherwise." Gail pulled back and let go two round punches to his right eye which dropped him in his chair. Then she poked him in the left eye with her long fingernail. Smorley tried to use his left hand to relieve the burning in his eye, as Gail pulled it off his face and shoved back two fingers till they dislocated and fractured. Smorley was near losing consciousness when Gail pulled the sap and snapped it at his jewels. Smorley puked all over his desk and then passed out.

While he was out, Gail secured the beast to his chair by tying his ankles and arms to the chair. After pulling his pants down, she threw some water in his face to bring him back. When Smorley's vision cleared, all he could see was a mad woman pulling on his tally-wacker and applying a buffalo skinning knife to his foreskin. Before Smorley could yell, the knife zipped across and the foreskin fell between Gail's fingers. Smorley went ballistic when he saw his tool bleeding and without a hood. "OOPS, I missed, better try another slice, heh?" "No, no, no, I'll sign the papers and give her the $10,000 she wants for her 10 years of marriage."

After helping Smorley sign the divorce papers and the $10,000 bank draft, Gail nonchalantly pulled the two hyperextended fingers down and said, "we'll send Doc Ross to care for your wounds, and till then, you'd better squeeze your sausage or you could bleed to death. Have more miserable days, cause I know Rebecca will have some good ones."

On their way back to the hospital Branch offered to exchange that buffalo knife for a more lady like jackknife—with a short blade. Gail started laughing. "So, did I do OK?" "I gave you the lead and you did the job of getting the papers and the bank draft signed. You done good. But, in the future, why don't we go straight to the tally-wacker. A simple circumcision certainly brings out the shock in a man's face and yields immediate results, heh?" "For sure!"

Just before supper, Branch sent a telegram to Anson Aiken in Pueblo, asking the current status of his three racehorses. The answer came back…….. "The stallion can do the quarter mile in 20 seconds, one filly can do it in 22 seconds. The second can only do it in 24 seconds. The first two are yours for another $1,000 each. The slow filly is yours without any more money, or I'll refund you your $1,000. Please advise, A. A."

Before sending a reply, Gail said, "knowing Anson, he's hoping you don't want that second filly. I say take her for breeding stock."

Enclosed is a $2,100 voucher for all three horses and the cost of their transfer by railroad to Waco, Tx c/o Marshal B. West.

With the end of the day at hand, the Duo had just enough time to ride out to the ranch for Zeb's supper and an evening at home.

***

CHAPTER 9

Tale of two Lives

With their lives so busy, the Duo decided to prepare an agenda for tomorrow. In the early morning, after breakfast, they rode to town and woke-up PF. "You're off for the next two days. Go fishing, go find some woman, or do something different for a change. We'll be spending the night and we'll see you tomorrow night." "Well, Ok. Guess I'll go fishing with my girlfriend and—never mind. Oh, Pappy will likely show up as he does every day, I think he wants to talk to you."

"Now, let's review our lists. Gail you make arrangements with Pastor Sutter for a morning wedding. Then make reservations at Sylvia's

Diner for a wedding meal and reception. We then meet for dinner. In the afternoon we buy our rings, and you take off to find a wedding dress, which I presume will take all afternoon. My list includes getting invitations printed and start addressing the envelopes. Afterwards, I'll send a telegraph to Denver at your old college advertising for a racehorse trainer. At the same time, I'll talk to Joshua about Randy again."

With things quiet in town, Branch headed to the telegraph to send his advertisement to Denver. Afterwards, Joshua said, "my wife and I would be proud to see our son enter the horse business as a racing jockey. Randy is so happy that it's almost ridiculous. When does he start work?" "As soon as my three racehorses arrive from Pueblo." Afterwards, he looked at Gail's list of invited guests: Cindy and Carl Otis, her college lady friend, Roger Whitmore, Marc Burton, the ranch workers, and four of the neighboring ranchers. Branch's list consisted of Captain Ennis of Denver, Sheriff Watson of Durango, Sheriff McBride of La Junta, Sheriff McBain of Pueblo, Sheriff Watkins of Colorado

Springs, the three members of his marshal squad in Denver, his parents and two brothers in Durango, and of course, the Martin family, Pappy and PF. Once he realized this came to +- 45 guests if they all came, he then ordered 50 invitations with the text as written by Gail.

Getting back to the office, Pappy was waiting on the porch. "What's new Pappy?" "Can we talk a bit?" "Sure, come on in. What's up?" "I'm bored to death, at 62 I don't have a darn thing to do. I don't want to go back to Denver and well........." "Well what would you like to do." "I'd like to be PF's deputy and the regular overnight jailer. I would take the back room and PF could get married, and live in a regular house—and that's my story, which PF was afraid to tell you." "Well you two nitwits, that's a fantastic idea. You'll get the same benefits as PF and welcome aboard. You can start working when PF says so, and by the way, I never thanked you for saving Gail. Thank you and I'll never forget."

When Gail arrived, they moseyed over to Sylvia's Diner for dinner. Gail said, "Sylvia is preparing a medium roast beef round and a chicken pie casserole dinner for our reception along with pie-a-la-mode. To meet your approval, that's what we are having for dinner today." "That's a great idea." "While we're waiting how did things go with Pastor Sutter?" "Fine, everything is set." "Now I sent my ad and we just hired our jockey. I ordered 50 invitations, but many of those need to be notified by telegram today." "That's ok, you do that this afternoon, and we'll still send an invitation according to tradition."

The meal was delicious, and Branch approved the two main dishes. Branch left a deposit of $150 to cover for dinner plus and open bar of beer and Doctor Pepper during the reception. After dinner, the Duo walked straight to the jeweler. A set of yellow gold wedding bands were chosen. While the teller was wrapping them, Branch saw a separate tray of shiny sparkling white things on gold rings. Branch asked, "what are those?" "Those are diamond engagement rings. They are rather pricey but certainly coruscated. How much is the big one?" "$800."

Branch picks it up and places it on Gail's finger. "Do you like it?" "Why of course, but it's rather expensive!" "Shush, remember what we agreed about money. The lady will wear it to go; no need to wrap this one."

Before walking to the dress maker, Gail planted a passionate kiss onto her 'husband to be,' letting him know of her appreciation for his personal gift. Looking at the shiny on her finger she said, "forever?" "Yes, forever!"

Branch then went back to the telegraph office to send at least 30 notices and invitations of their wedding in 10 days. On his way back to the office, he stopped at a haberdashery and ordered a half dozen books on racing—especially on short distance sprint racing. The one book that was on the shelf, light duty racing saddles, was taken with him to review and show to his leather worker at the ranch. Stepping back on the boardwalk, Branch saw a typical scene grow into an all-out attack.

Two ladies stepped out of a mercantile and the three bums reacted. One arrogant wise-ass got up and went to the younger of the ladies, grabbed her rear end and squeezed it till the young gal yelped out. All three started hooting and hollering as the gal's dad came out of the mercantile carrying a 50-pound bag of flour on his shoulder. When he saw his daughter being man handled, he used the only thing he had to fend off the attack—he threw his bag of flour at the lead miscreant. The result was an all-out fist fight against the older man.

Branch stepped up, forcibly kicked the apparent aggressor in the rear-end and shoved his pants into his butthole. The second one got the butt end of his Mare's Leg against his nose and the third got the muzzle of his shotgun pointed at his crotch. Branch added, "give me a reason, you idiot. Now, you're all under arrest, a week in jail will hopefully smarten you up, and that will give us time to see if you have any warrants on your 'pinheads.'"

After getting the victim to apply the manacles, Branch asked, "I don't see a firearm in your wagon. Why not?" "Can't afford one, life is still day by day on the homestead—have no money till the crops come in this summer. Right now we live on Mister Washburn's credit. Branch looked at Sam, the mercantile owner, and simply nodded. As he was walking the three troublemakers to the jail, Winston Brubaker was walking out with a new double barrel shotgun with several boxes of shells and a credit slip for $500—c/o The Benefactor Fund.

With three clients in jail, Pappy was happily called in to start working as jailer. Branch had plenty of time to do one more errand and went to a man's garment store and bought his dress suit. A dark grey pinstripe suit with a light grey vest, a new hat and new boots. Along with the dressy suit he bought several work clothes for both the ranch and the marshal service.

Gail finally arrived with a large box. "This is my dress, a bit revealing but I'm sure you and our guests will like it. If necessary, I have a shawl to match." "Ok, let me see?" "Oh no, you cannot see me in this dress till I walk down the aisle." "Well that reeks blue babies, heh?"

That night, Pappy went home, and the Duo were the overnight jailers and available lawmen. Under two lamps, the Duo addressed all the

238 Richard M Beloin MD

invitations. Just as they were setting up their cots for the night, someone came pounding on the door. "Marshal come quick, a local cowboy caught a flimflam man cheating at cards, but the arrogant cardsharp is threatening to kill the cowboy or anyone who tries to stop him from escaping."

The Duo went to work. Running with the informant, they went straight to Swanton's Saloon. Gail was sent to the back door as Branch entered thru the front batwing doors. There it was! A Mexican standoff. The cowboy and the dandy had pistols out with hammers pulled back. Branch slowly walked to the cowboy and said, "stand down son, you done good to hold him in place, now sit down and let me take over." The cowboy was more than happy to comply. As soon as Branch pulled out his Mare's Leg, the cowboy holstered his Colt and backed off.

"Now folks, who is going to tell me what is going on?" "I will," said the same cowboy. We were playing five-card-draw—three up and two down. This idiot, with already four queens showing, pulls a 5th queen. Duuuuh, the rest is history, marshal." "I see, well mister flimflam, pull your sleeve up and put the gun away. The local punishment for cheating at cards is three days in jail then one day to get out of town for good." The man refused to put his mini pistol away. Branch finally said, what are you going to do? Shoot a US Marshal over a $5 pot. I'll tell you now, even if you shoot me, I will shoot you dead with my shotgun. So put it away, and come along." The cheat finally surrendered his pistol, but Branch made him empty his pockets of cash to repay the other card players. As they turned around, Gail had her pistol to some hombre's head as she said, "I think this one was the flimflam's spotter and bodyguard. He pulled his hog leg on you, but never got to pull the hammer since his nostril was full of my pistol barrel." Branch's only words were, "for sure, heh?"

The spotter had $79 in his pockets, and they gave him back $25 for future train tickets, the rest of the money was to pay for meals and lodging for those three days in the hoosegow. Finally, the Duo made their beds and got a full night's sleep after just a goodnight kiss.

In the morning, with a fresh pot of coffee made, Pappy showed up. "We're going to Sylvia's for breakfast." They hadn't been sitting down for long when Randy arrived with an urgent telegram. "Marshal, my pa says that I need to wait for an answer." The Duo read the gram together.

> Wife and I are graduating from horse training school STOP
> Am presently interviewing at McGalloway stables in Dallas STOP
> Would like to apply for a job at your ranch STOP
> Both our families live in Waco STOP
> Can we come for an interview STOP
> RSVP The Irvings

The Duo looked at each other and smiled. "BINGO" said Gail. The answer simply said:

> Come tomorrow on first daily train STOP
> Enclosed is $20 voucher for expenses STOP

Tell Mister McGalloway, NO THANKS, Going home STOP

Will meet you at railroad depot STOP RSVP

Marshal West c/o The Circle W Ranch

With that settled, their hash and poached eggs arrived. "Sounds like we are getting a long-term team. What do we offer them for salaries and benefits?" Branch pondered the question and finally said, "starting pay, $60 each will give them a nice monthly sum of $120 plus medical expenses and a life insurance policy. Now for lodging, that's a different matter. As a married couple, we can't put them in a bunkhouse."

Gail smiled and finally said, "I'm beginning to really know you. When you bring up a subject, you're like an attorney. You never ask a question or breach a subject without knowing the answer or the solution. So come out with it!"

"Well, Ok. It's what Otis said at the settlement. 'You never lose a key employee because of money or housing.' That's why the Ashburns have their own house on the ranch. What it comes to is that when a single worker takes on a woman, significant-other or wife, if he is an essential worker, then we need to provide family housing. Now I look at our young workers and I see several that will be eligible since not a one of them is a 'sloth' in their appearance." "This is so true, but how do we deal with it?"

"With their verbal personal guarantee that they will stay with us for at least five years, we will build them a furnished house with indoor plumbing and a small barn." "I see, so we'll end up with our own village and I'll have lady friends to visit or go shopping with, heh?" "For sure, dear!" "So what will that cost us?" "Oh, it's finally OUR money, heh?" Yes, but only if you make it to the altar next week."

*

That night, they again slept at the marshal's office and again had to forgo intimate events with a jail full of customers. The next morning, Branch told PF that they would be going back to the ranch after meeting with potential trainers. Back at Sylvia's Diner, Branch dared to bring up a sensitive matter. "We seem to have too many sticks in the fire, and it is a big fire. We have a big business that is heading for expansion, and the town needs a strong lawman presence. I just can't see how we can continue to burn the candle at both ends. One of us has to 'own' the ranch and the other has to 'own' the marshal's responsibility." "Wow, I was afraid that this topic would come up. So to help us decide, I want to make it clear that I have certain priorities that have come about recently. First, I want to be with you, I want you in my life, and what you want is what I want—nothing else comes close to matter anymore. Secondly is my love of horses and the ranch, and third is upholding the law. So, how do we move forward."

"This is my plan, assuming it is accepted by Captain Ennis. PF and Pappy need to be official full time Deputy US Marshals, I need to go to part-time service. I need to be seen on the job at least two afternoons a week plus on duty all day Saturday and Saturday night. I need to be available to do man hunts, solve robberies and major criminal events in the town's jurisdiction on a 'as needed basis.' The remainder of the time, I will spend on the ranch as co-manager next to you, and concentrate my efforts on horse racing and crop farming—while you manage the remainder of the ranch's activities."

"I can agree with that under one and only one condition." "I agree!" "Hold on, better hear me out. The condition is, that I spend Saturday and Saturday night at your side, watching your back and protecting my only concern—and that's not negotiable." "That's not a problem since you are still a US Deputy Marshal. We'll just put you on temporary service and be paid $10 by the day. So in anticipation, I prepared a written request for these changes and after breakfast, we can stop at the telegraph office to send our request to Captain Ennis."

After a full breakfast of pancakes, bacon, home-fries, and two full pots of coffee with a cinnamon bun, the Duo checked the train schedule and realized they had two hours to spend before the job applicants arrived. After sending off their telegram to Denver, Gail suggested they visit the Bumstead Saddle and

Harness shop—parents of Barney, their harness maker. Entering, Barney's dad walked up to them and said, "hello Gail, how are you and this must be the man that everyone is talking about." After introductions were finished, Branch informed the elder, "I'm going to build a new division at the Circle W. We are adding short distance horse racing and need a functional but very light saddle. Opening the shop manual on different saddles, he showed the owner the pictures of different racing saddles. Gail was also looking on and finally said, "I like that one!"

Mister Bumstead said, "that's the standard US Cavalry saddle. Cheap to make, yet a leather seat and strong stirrups. It was made for short distances as a patrol would not travel for days. It is really ideal with the strong stirrups that allow a jockey to stand up off the saddle's seat." "Is this something that your son could manufacture himself." "Of course, I would give him a one-day course and he would have no problems in making them. It is actually a good choice, because as a horse grows out, it would only take minor changes to accommodate the horse's change in size and weight." "How much for the course?" "Heck, it's all in the family. There is no charge, as long as if he cannot keep up with the demand, that you send us the extra business. Ok?" "Done, and thanks."

Coming out of the saddle shop, Gail suggested a cold drink before the train arrived. They walked in the nearest saloon and Branch ordered a beer, but Gail surprised him by ordering a "Doctor Pepper." Branch asked, "what in blazes is that?" It is a sweet soda pop similar to a sarsaparilla, but locally made. This is a local product that is predicted to go nationwide." When Gail's choice arrived, Branch took a sip and said, "yep, this is going to be a keeper and Waco will gain national recognition. Barkeep, change my order and give me one of these, please."

Sitting on the saloon's porch rocking chairs, while drinking their refreshments, three arrogant loud mouths, walked by. Branch's marshal badge was hidden by his vest and the cowboys started hooting and hollering. "Well lookie-ere, a full-grown sissy drinking a sodie-pup. Ha, ha, ha." Gail simply looked at Branch fully knowing that this was not going to be a good day for these idiots. To make matters worse, one of the sycophants had to add his own insult by kicking Branch's boot and saying, "hey sissy-pants, we're talking to you." Gail, trying to avert an all-out response added, "boys, don't you know that if you wake up a grizzly, you can expect to get your ass chewed up. Best to walk away, or apologize to the man if you want to keep your front teeth." "What, that pathetic slouch is going to put us down? Get up, act like a man, and put up your best, dickhead."

Branch had had it. Without any warning he dropped the heel of his boot onto the mouthy one's toes and knew that he heard bones snap. The toadie fell to the porch floor moaning and holding his foot. Then the brawl started. Branch had no hold back, he preferred to deal with them with fists, that they were used to, for if he pulled his Mare's Leg, blood would be spilled. Branch took control of the situation with several punches that claimed several teeth.

When all three were subdued, manacles were applied, and Branch then showed his US

Marshal badge. The one fella that had never spoke started laughing and said, "you flaming idiots, you picked a fight with a US Marshal, I can't believe I go around with d--b f---s. I need some new friends with some active marbles between their ears."

Arriving at the jail, the three were thrown in a cell. Branch said to Pappy, "charge them with breaking the peace and keep them a couple of days." "According with the town ordinance, they can get a maximum of four days if you want." "Naw, their pride is hurt, two days is enough."

Standing at the train platform, the Duo saw two young well-built and well-dressed individuals. The gal was beyond comely and the guy was a winsome. Gail softly said, "now, there is evidence of good gene inheritance, and I don't mean blue jeans, heh?" "Yep, for sure, for sure, for sure, as he felt a poke in his side."

The Duo stepped up as the man said, "hello marshal, we are Toby and Jane Irving and we are looking for Otis and Gail Woods." "I'm Gail, and the marshal is my fiancé and husband to be, as well as co-owner. My uncle Otis has retired and lives in Denver for medical care." Branch took over and said, "if you're hungry, let's go to Sylvia's Diner for dinner and we can talk."

After placing their orders of a cold roast beef sandwich, Gail said, "while we're waiting, give us your background and why you are here today. Toby started, "we were both raised in Waco but at different parts of town and in separate school districts, so we never met socially. After graduating at age 16, we both spent three years at odd jobs to gather enough money to go to college. While we were in line to register in the horsemanship division, this woman was behind me complaining that her feet hurt standing for this long. So we started talking, and found out we lived only ten streets away in Waco. Then to make it surreal, we were both applying for the horsemanship college, she was specializing in harness training and me in horse racing. Well not to divulge personal events, we fell in love and actually got married a week ago after the courses finished. During our week, we have been hunting for a job since graduation is in four days. We were leaving Anson Aiken's AA Ranch in Pueblo when our guidance counselor sent us a telegram about your ad. Our next stop was the McGalloway Stables when we made contact with you, and here we are." Gail asked, "are you interested in either place?" Jane took over, "Either place would be good for Toby, but I would not be able to use my harness training skills, these are solely racing establishments." "Well, Ma'am, we need someone to help our trainers with harness training. We have two trainers; the younger actually does the saddle training while the older one does harness training. That older trainer needs help with harness training. So, Gail will tell you everything about the ranch and I'll discuss horse racing afterwards."

Even talking thru lunch, Gail covered the basics of the Circle W Ranch—with emphasis on the different harness needs from buggy riding to heavy duty draft horse jobs and presenting Barnie as the resident harness maker. After lunch Branch added, "I want to start a horse training program. I have purchased three two+ yearlings from the AA ranch, we have several 2-year old colts and fillies that we can select for training, we need to build a quarter mile racetrack with a graded raceway, and we need to build our own racing saddles—plus I'm going to be gone often as a US Marshal and you will have the responsibility of getting things going."

Gail broke in and said, "well what do you think, are you interested. If you are, we can talk about wages and then we'll show you the ranch."

Jane was fidgeting and looking bug eyed at her husband. Toby then added, "we may only be married a week, but I know Jane wants this job, and so do I."

Branch looked at Gail and got the nod. "Any idea what you wish for wages." "No sir, we'll take whatever you offer us," as Jane was nodding in approval. Gail said, we now pay both trainers $75 a month with room and board in the bunkhouse." "We can offer you $60 as starting pay." We can live on $60 a month since we can live with family in town." "No, no, no, that's $60 each and it includes a lodging allotment of $25 a month, since as a married couple, you cannot live in the bunkhouse. It also includes three meals a day at the cook shack."

Toby interrupted, "but sir, that is way too much money for newbies." Gail jumped in, "we know you are newbies, but you have training, you are the personalities that will blend with our great workers, and we know you will work out." Branch added, and there is more, "we just recently decided that we needed to provide housing for our married couples when at least one works on the ranch. So, in a month or so, if you work out and wish to stay with us for five years, as by your word, we will build you your own new furnished home on the ranch, with inside plumbing, a separate barn, firewood, and heating coal. All as included benefits to your wages. So, what do you say, how about giving us a try and sign on?" Jane lost it and started crying uncontrollably. Once she regained control, she finally spoke. "There is no doubt that Toby and I will give you 110%, but there may be a problem." "What on earth could interfere with these plans." "What on earth happens with all these plans and our commitment to you, if I become pregnant."

The Duo looked at each other and broke out laughing. To the Irving's dismay, they just kept laughing. Finally, Gail gathered herself enough to say, "can you imagine the look on our workers' faces when they start seeing that 'bump' grow out of your work jeans—yeah a real catastrophe, for sure."

Branch saw that the Irving's were lost so he finally spoke. "Mark my words, for I'll never repeat it. Please do not try to avoid pregnancy to save your job. If you are gifted with children, so be it. We will never abandon you no matter how many pregnancies you have. Your salary will continue without any interruption. If you are healthy and your doctor allows you to work, then do so till you know it is time to stop. After the birth, only return to work when your doctor says it is Ok and you are ready. Just remember, we will all manage."

Gail added, "we hope to have a family, and we decided to build other homes for married workers, heck, we'll probably end up with a village of families with children. Won't that be great?"

Toby looked at Jane and got the clear nod. "We'd be happy to sign on. Where do we sign?" "A shake of hands is all we need." After the formality, Branch said, "let's rent a buggy and we'll show you the ranch and you can meet your co-workers. Afterwards, we are putting you up at the Princess Waco Hotel with included meals, for two nights as your honeymoon gift from us. Afterwards, I know you are heading back to Denver, so when can you come back and start work?"

"We can be back in a week; we want that certificate since we worked for it. For your information, when we were at the AA Ranch in Pueblo, we found out that they were giving a week's course on training racehorses. We wonder if we should take it before coming to Waco?" "Certainly, of course, how appropriate in an opportune time. How much is the course?" "We have enough money left, so we can pay for it. The course is only $20." "Nonsense, there is lodging and food expenses. I want you both to take it. While looking at Jane, Branch adds, "you never know when it may also be useful to help Toby. Here is $200 to cover all course expenses, plus some extra for you to buy some work duds, personal items and each a gun for self-defense. Now let's go for a ride to the ranch."

*

The easy ride allowed more bonding with the new workers. As they arrived at the homestead, the Irvings were in total aww seeing the many buildings and two new buildings under construction—the blacksmith shop and second barn. The group disembarked and started walking along the pastures to look at the hundreds of horses. They were shown each building, met every worker, and Jane was already chatting with Annette. The one meeting that was impressive is when Ansel was told that he was getting a helper. Benny started objecting till Ansel, the harness trainer, said, "Benny, you don't need any help, heck the whisperer does 80% of your work, I'm the one who needs help. Welcome, Ma'am, I'd be glad to work with you." "Please call me Jane, and may I call you Ansel?" "Be honored if you did."

Before heading back to town, they rode besides the Ashburn's home and Gail said, "next door is where we will build yours." They then rode by the fields reserved for growing hay and the new sections being cultivated for new crops. On their way back to town, Toby said, "I spotted where we need to build the racetrack—it is next to the new barn." "Good we'll work on that when you return, now it's time to get you registered in your hotel, I'll then send a telegram to A. Aiken to reserve two spots in the next class of racehorse training, and then we'll have supper with you before we go back to the ranch."

As agreed, they met in the hotel lobby at 6PM. The Irvings had up- scaled their attire to match the restaurant's décor and ambiance. After ordering some tenderloin steaks with baked potatoes and all the fixings, they found it very easy to cover any subject at hand. To avoid talking about work, they asked why they should buy a gun on a ranch close to town in 1892. Branch was first to answer.

"This is still a violent land. We expect all our workers to be able to defend themselves and our ranch. We don't want ladies to go to town by themselves and we want them all able to handle a pistol, rifle and shotgun. Right now, times are finally getting peaceful, but there are so many outlaws looking for a quick way to make money, and a beautiful woman hostage is a way to make money and relieve their natural urges. I hope you buy each a Webley Bulldog in 44 with a belt holster or a shoulder holster. Plus it is small enough to fit in a reticule. Remember Jane, you are fresh bait for predators. You cannot make yourself look like a 'booglin.'"

Jane looked puzzled as Gail said "short, fat and ugly. He's told me the same thing some time ago." Once the laughter subsided, the meals arrived. The evening went well, and the Duo realized that they were making their first friends. After the evening rounded up, the couples went their own way till they would meet again in a few weeks.

***

CHAPTER 10

The Wedding and Settling Down

After a short ride to the ranch, they rode to the barn and unsaddled their horses. Zeke came out of the bunkhouse to greet them. "The barn concrete flooring is being poured tomorrow and we'll etch the surface to make it non-kid." "Good, my only suggestion is to hold the stall partitioning till you can speak to Toby since he'll likely want specific stalls and pens for racehorses." "Good, idea. I'll hold the carpenters after the shell and roof is up till Toby arrives."

The Duo then moved to the ranch house. Sitting in the parlor, Branch asks, "so what is on the agenda for the week" "We are getting married on Saturday, and since we are ready, you are free till you hear from some of your invitees." "Well, in that case, I'm spending time with all of the ranch workers. I will start with Barney in the morning since I want to get started on choosing a racing saddle."

Gail added, "I need to set up the books for payroll and general accounting. Also, I need to write letters to some of our past suppliers of young breeding stock. It is time to find one-year-olds for training, and 3-years old mares for breeding." "Where do you find such animals?"

"In the past, we bought from ranchers and homesteaders as private sales. That way we don't compete against commercial outfits that raise similar horses."

In the AM, The Duo went to breakfast. Afterwards, Branch followed Barney to his shop. Barney started, "last night I had dinner with mom and dad. The subject of building a racing saddle came up. After dinner, we researched this subject in dad's extensive library of texts and periodicals. The upshot is that a McClellan saddle is not the answer for it is really a riding saddle that comes one size and requires the horse to fit in the saddle. The McClellan weighs +-20-30 pounds and the Western saddle weighs 20-60 pounds. Now the light and flat racing saddle we have designed will weigh +- 10 pounds. The specs include:

1. Short stirrups. This allows the rider to stand up over the horse's withers and also allows the horse's legs and shoulders more freedom of movement to move faster.
2. A longer saddle with a stronger saddle tree to which the stirrups are attached.
3. A flat pommel and cantle, unlike the standard riding saddles.
4. Longer and wider side flaps to protect the rider's lower legs.
5. Flip up bridle blinkers to prevent sideways distractions.
6. Hackamore bridle without mouth bit.
7. Saddle blanket to match the new smaller saddle size."

"Amazing, I really like it. So, who will make them." "My dad's factory. They will put a team on this and will make varied sizes that will fit a one-year-old up to a four-year-old. Like the riding saddle assortment we have in the tack room for training, we'll now have a similar number of racing saddles for Toby to choose from the new barn's tack room." "Great work, order the multiple sizes. Now let's move on to harnesses."

"The leather we use is full grain steer hide that is vegetable tanned but not treated with wax, oils, or sanded down. That preserves the strength of the natural fibers. Leather thickness is based on 'ounce' nomenclature. One-ounce leather is 1/64 inch thick. We don't use any leather less than 10- ounce which is 3/16 inch. When you build a draft horse's harness, we are now talking about 12-16-ounce leather—or whatever we can get."

"Our harnesses fall in one of four categories. Breast strap, neck collar/hames, breeching or non-breeching." "Breeching means?" "A wide strap that passes around the hindquarters and allows a horse to stop or reverse."

"Now, you can imagine that a buggy harness only requires a breast strap, whereas work horses need the strength of a neck collar with attached hames hardware. Now a harness for plowing does not need a breeching strap since you cannot back up a plow—so they tell me."

"So what do you do when you don't have the correct leather thickness for a certain harness?" "Thanks to the sewing machine I sew several thinner pieces together. The traces are such examples since the bulk of the tension is in the final harness connection to the payload."

"How much do you charge for harnesses. A light duty buggy harness can go for $90, whereas a draft horse's harness can go as high as $250. You do realize, unless refused, that no harness horse goes off this ranch without its own fitted harness and the price is added to the horse's value." Branch was looking at a new harness and grabbed it to heft it up but failed to lift it off the floor. "How much do harnesses weigh?" A lightweight buggy harness might weigh 50 pounds, but that draft horse one you just tried to lift weighs +-130 pounds."

"Let's go over your tools." Barney explained what the hand tools did and the several punch/ rivet presses and sewing machines. When Barney got to the newest addition, he said, "this is the most important tool in the shop and saves the full-time labor of a helper." "What does it do?" "Watch." Barney takes a 12 ounce hide, places it in the machine, sets a dial on 2 and starts peddling with his feet. The machine moved the hide, cut a perfect 2-inch strap of leather from one edge of the hide to the other. "And as you can see, it is perfectly straight."

"Well Barney, I'm impressed. You are well set up and you do good work. I will assume that you do not need a helper at this point?" "No, and even if the ranch expands, I think I can handle the workload as long as I don't have to build time consuming saddles."

The next day, the Duo again went to breakfast. Afterwards, Branch says to Zeke, "today, I would like to work with you to see the work you do." "Great, follow me, I can use your help."

Entering the barn, a dozen or more horses were just finishing chomping their hay and grain down. "When do you start your day, Zeke? Some of these horses were in the pasture and yet they have all been fed and watered." "I start to feed them an hour before breakfast so I can get them harnessed right after breakfast."

So for the next hour, we will be harnessing work horses. The first two are the Belgian team for plowing. After the two men hefted the massive harness on a 19-hand massive horse, Branch said, "how in hell can you harness this team yourself?" "Well, I cheat and wait for the cropboys to arrive. Yet, I have all the other crop teams harnessed to include the horses for disc harrowing, finish harrowing, and the manure spreader. Once those are off to work, we muck the stalls." With some 40 horses that spent the night in the barn, it took the two men an hour to muck all the stalls. "Afterwards, I harness and hitch the team to haul the water and snack wagon for the 10AM break. Once this was done, Branch filled the water tank as Zeke picked up the snacks prepared by Zeb.

"Why are those ten horses still in the barn?" "Those are the ailing ones that need treatments two or three times a day." "Like what conditions?" "Well since you asked, here are the common maladies that I treat with oral meds, poultices, potions, salves, drainage, and other natural remedies all provided by our vet:

1. Founder or laminitis. A lame horse caused by too much carbohydrates in the diet. It is an inflammation of the tissues (lamina) that attach the hoof to the bone.
2. Colic.
3. Arthritis.
4. Respiratory infections'
5. Pigeon fever.
6. Strangles.
7. Sunburnt skin."

"Did you say oral meds?" "Yes, we use a lot of phenylbutazone for pain relief and banamine for fever relief."

By the noon dinner, Branch was exhausted. The afternoon was filled with one job after another. Zeke never stopped and at times was seen running back to the pasture to get some more work horses. Finally at 5PM, Branch was struggling to replace a harness on the assigned rack as he said, "that's it Zeke. Enough is enough. You're not a young man to do this work. This is insane. Why didn't you ask for a helper?"

"Because I was afraid that I would end up with some young whipper-snapper that thinks he knows everything, but is totally useless when it comes down to doing the work." "Not so if you choose your own worker." "I agree I need help and I already have someone in mind, but there may be a problem. His name is Oscar Sands. He is my sister's boy who is a bit slow, but is a genius handling horses. He lives on his own doing odd jobs in town. Yet, he is trustworthy, strong and a very pleasant 20-year-old that is also a good friend of mine. I just know he will work out in the barn, fit in the bunkhouse, and even might add some horse training skills." "Stop, of course, bring him in, and let Gail assign him wages and benefits."

That evening, Branch told Gail about Zeke's nephew. Gail said, "this will be a good worker for Zeke. I know of the fella, and I've never heard of any complaints about him." "Good. Now tomorrow I'm spending time with the two trainers in the morning and the smithy/farrier in the afternoon. I need to watch these two workers, since I really cannot help them like I did with Zeke."

Again, after breakfast, Branch followed Ansel to the barn. Ansel would take the trainee of the morning and harness him. Then he would bring the horse to the training yard where several wagons were stored. Once hitched to its designated wagon, Ansel would provide the necessary commands and guide the horse to the main road for a short trip back and forth several times.

After two hours, Ansel went back to the barn for his second trainee. Of course, Zeke had already harnessed the next horse and would unharness the one which had just finished his lesson. This continued all day as Benny and Obadiah were working horses in the exercise ring.

At 4PM, Ansel brought a team of 18-hand Belgians to a special training area. The traces were attached to a concrete block with chains. "What in blazes is this for?" "We do competition horse pulling at least four times a year in town. These two horses can each pull 8,000 pounds. But put them together as a team and they can drag 20,000 pounds. We win enough to add $1,000 annually to the till. Plus some extra play money from individual wagers." "Fantastic, make sure you tell me of the next pull, cause I'm coming! I'm sure, that these are pleasant days for the ranch workers, heh?"

After dinner, Branch headed to the new blacksmith/farrier shop with Buck McKenzie. After a tour of the new digs, Buck gave Branch a show of how he turned a standard bar stock into a finished horseshoe. With a red-hot piece of steel, a handheld sledgehammer, and a well-equipped anvil, Buck impressed Branch with his talent. Buck explained that with a forge and an anvil, the smithy could make whatever piece of steel was needed. Branch was looking at the anvil and finally said, "I always knew that the anvil had two parts, the front horn and the flat top. But what is that square hole in the flat top?"

"That's the Hardy hole to hold Hardy tools." To demonstrate, Buck inserted a square based chisel in the Hardy hole. Then he placed a small steel rod on top of the chisel and hit the rod with his hammer. The cut was perfect, and Branch understood. He then looked at the dozen different Hardy tools that were in the tray.

Moving on, "talk to me about horseshoes." "We shoe horses to prevent excessive hoof wear, gain traction, and protect the hoof from splitting. We re-shoe them whenever the shoe is worn, and we reset them if the shoe gets loose. I make two kinds of shoes. The regular shoe has a shallow nail groove on the right and left side of the shoe. The Rim shoe has a deeper nail groove and goes all around the shoe from tip to tip for traction as in work and racing horses."

"Good to know. Now how do you shoe the rear shoes without getting kicked?" "Being alone when I shoe a horse, the front hoof is not a problem. I hold it between my legs and do the work. The rear leg is the problem. I secure it with three straps, one to hold the leg bent at the knee, and two to prevent rear and forward motion. Even then, some of these stallions manage to get some flesh off me—that's the nature of the beast."

That evening, in their parlor, Branch said, "at supper, Gary said they were planning a supervised breeding of one of the mares in heat. Apparently breeding is the responsibility of the foreman and the wrangler. Old Zeke never told me about this added responsibility like I suspect there are many other jobs he does from day to day." "Have you ever seen a stallion set a mare and inseminate her?" "No, I guess I only saw cattle breeding." "Well, it is an experience, and I think I had better be with you to answer your questions since Gary and Zeke will have their hands full, literally and figuratively, and won't have time to answer your questions." And so the day would start with the first of many surprises.

*

At Gail's suggestion, Branch had a light breakfast. Arriving in the barn, the stallion was secured in his feeding station. When the mare arrived, the stallion in the neighboring stall was standing arched in an unnatural position. Branch did a double take, "what is that one doing?" Gail looked and said, "oh, he's upset that his buddy got the mare, so he's just spilling his seed, that's all." Branch tried to express an 'of course' remark but quickly decided he was in a hole and it was best to stop trying to dig his way out—so he shut up.

Once the mare was secured, the stallion was released from his station. Then the romancing started with neighing, rubbing, smelling, and even snipping. Once in full tumescence, the 'older' stallion mounted but his penis, although firm, was pointing 45 degrees at the ground. Zeke nonchalantly took hold of it to support it and the natural process continued. The stallion's last thrust nearly bent the mare in half. Branch was stupefied at the so-called natural process and added, "plus you told me that they will breed that mare daily for three days?" "Yes sir, and the insemination rate will be 95%

which justifies the extra attention over pasture breeding with its lower insemination rate."

After dinner, the Duo was sitting on their porch. Gail said, "today is Thursday and we are getting married on Saturday. I think it's time to tie up loose ends." Before Branch could ask more on the subject, a rider came down the access road. "Anyone riding at that speed has to be Randy."

Arriving in a huff, he stepped down and took the time to address the Duo, Marshal West and Woods. "I was at the depot delivering telegrams to some passengers when I saw three magnificent horses being guided out of the stockcar by a young gal and fella. The railroad ticket agent told me they were your horses. Are those the horses I'm supposed to ride and race?" "Why, I suspect you are right. So why don't you come over tonight look over the new racing saddle and get acquainted with these new horses.? I even suspect the new racing trainer will be here to meet you!"

After Randy left, the Duo looked at each other and just shrugged their shoulders. "I'm sure there must be a heck of a story behind that, if it's true the Irvings are here!" Sure as shooting, two hours later, Toby and Jane appeared on two saddled horses. Jane was trailing a filly as Toby was trailing the colt stallion and one filly.

After they arrived, Gail was totally blown over, "Branch, these are beautiful and well-developed Quarter horses, as I have ever seen. Toby added, "and built to race." Branch walked around, admiring the beautiful horseflesh, and showing a grin from ear to ear. Zeke arrived to take the horses to the barn as the Irvings were invited to sit and explain what they were doing here.

Toby started, "we had just finished the course provided by the AA ranch. We learned so much on how to progressively train these racehorses as well as important tips on nutrition, ailments, and very specific needs in supplements. We are ready to provide state of the art training and care of your horses."

Jane then added, "we were planning to return to Denver to get our certificates when Mister Aiken announced that he was shipping your horses today. Ironically, we were at the depot preparing to board our train to Denver when we saw the railroad stockman roughly jerk your horses about. When we confronted this person, with the railroad agent present, it was clear that he was drunk, and the agent fired him on the spot. Well to shorten the story, we became the attendants and rode with your horses—in the stockcar and here we are. Our families met us at the station to take our luggage and we are here ready to work."

Gail added, "we won't forget how you went the extra mile to guarantee the safe arrival of our new horses." Branch was next, "since you are here, let me bring you up to snuff on what we have accomplished in preparing for your arrival:

1. Our wrangler and trainers have selected a dozen two-year-old's as possible candidates for racing stock. You'll have to select the best specimens and move them into the new barn.

2. We are building a second barn and your racing horses will be housed in there. You need to meet with Zeke and the carpenters

to set up the stalls, tack room and other specifics. Plan on utilizing a dozen spots out of fifty and Zeke will use the balance.

3. Our foreman has been working with Buck, our blacksmith, to convert the frame of an old plow to a scraping back blade. This, along with harrows and a packing roller, is what you'll need to build the racetrack.

4. Our harness maker, Barney Bumstead, has been working with his dad at the family saddlery to build us a state-of-the-art true racing saddle that weighs +-10 pounds. He is now at the family shop working on that as we speak, and he is supposed to bring a prototype back here tonight. You'll get the chance to add your modifications before they make us a bunch to fit different size horses.

5. Tonight, you get a chance to meet your jockey since he's coming here after supper.

6. Saturday is our wedding, and like all our employees, you are invited. It's going to be a perfect time to socialize with our workers and several of the town folks we do business

with. Speaking of supper, shall we all step to the cook shack where we can talk some more about these preparations?"

＊

Two days later, the wedding day had arrived. Sitting in their parlor at daybreak, they were invaded by three ladies, Annette, Jane, and sister Cindy, with bags of stuff. Annette was the spokesperson, "not to be disrespectful of my boss, but you have an hour to bathe and change into your suit and get out of here. You can wait at the marshal's office but be sure to be at the church no later than 11:45 for Gail is walking in at high noon. We need all morning to get your bride ready, so suck up your coffee and get moving. Us ladies are having some breakfast, and we are going to work after the dishes are done." "I don't understand what could possibly take three hours just to put her wedding gown on?" "We need to find something old, something new, something blue, she needs to bathe, we need to do her hair, apply facial powders, and possibly make alterations to her dress and veil. So enough talk, get busy." Gail simply smiled and said, "I love you so, partner."

Waiting at the marshal's office, there was a knock and PF opened the door. There stood an elderly couple. Branch got up and grabbed his mom who was crying uncontrollably. His dad had a tear ready to drip when they hugged. PF quietly stepped outside to give them some privacy. After the pleasantries were done with, Branch started, "I've made my way and I'm finally wealthy. More important, I've met the love of my life and I know you'll love her. I am now moving away from the US Marshal Service and I am the co-owner of a horse ranch where we raise riding horses, work horses, cow-punching horses and racing horses. Now how about you two, and my brothers."

"Your brothers and their families are in the Silver City area of New Mexico. They could not handle the stone dust caused by hydraulic equipment, so they both moved to New Mexico to work in open-pit copper mines. Because of their mechanical and dexterous abilities, they are both steam shovel operators with a good pay. The wives and children are well settled down and they will never return to Durango."

"I'm going to retire in a few months, and I don't know what I'll be doing to spend my time since I've always worked for a living and never had a hobby. Your mom has had a very bad six months when her five grandchildren moved to New Mexico. She went thru a severe melancholy and cried unconsolably for weeks. Now things are settling down but after being with family all our lives, we are now alone in our senior years. I worry for your mother."

"Why don't you sell your house and move to Silver City with the grandchildren?" "Because, our house is worth $1,000. We have another $1,000 in the bank. Silver City is an expensive place to live with all the gold, silver, and copper. The houses start at $3,000 and the cost of living is so high that we cannot afford to move there."

"Stop, say no more. Sell your house, send all your belongings and furniture, move to Waco, and I'll build you a new home on the ranch. It will cost you nothing. I'll even include a barn, heating coal, cooking firewood and indoor plumbing. Plus, twice a year, I will pay your fare by train to Silver City and include hotel fees and meals for one week. You will be able to keep with your grandchildren's lives."

Branch's mom finally spoke, "why would you do such a thing, and no one can afford such expenses." "Because you took care of me for 18 years, and it is now my turn to take care of you and trust me, I can afford it money wise. Besides, dad can work during the crop harvest and you will also be busy with my own children."

Branch's dad had been quiet but finally said, "I'm not saying no, but we'll talk about this after your honeymoon. Meanwhile, we are spending a week in Waco to get acquainted, and will wait for your return with our daughter in law before we make up our minds." "Fine, but you are staying in our ranch house and taking your meals at the cook shack. You need to get to know the people who work here and would be your neighbors. You can also take day trips to town to get acquainted, as you called it, heh?"

*

Branch managed to be at church by 11:30 with PF, his best man. Branch was watching the guests arrive and was shocked at the attendance. More than invited guests were showing up, especially amongst local people. Of out-of-towners, Branch recognized Captain Ennis and the Missus, and all of the local lawmen he met during his time as a bounty hunter. After the church was full, a silence and stillness hovered over the guests. Suddenly, the minister joined Branch and PF. Without warning, the organist blasted out the wedding march, all heads turned to the church entrance as Otis walked in with his niece on his arm. PF heard Branch whisper, "gorgeous, simply ravishing, how did I ever manage to land this catch?"

The remainder of the ceremony was a blur until he heard the minister say, "you may now kiss your bride." The newlyweds, by tradition were first to walk out of church, and stand by the door to greet all their guests. Once that was done, PF announced that everyone was invited to Sylvia's Diner for a reception to include refreshments and dinner. As everyone was walking to the diner, one of PF's friends yelled out, "what's for dinner, horse meat?" "No, nothing that fancy, just clabber!"

As guests entered the diner, men were given a mug of cold beer and the ladies were offered an open bottle of Doctor Pepper with an upside-down drinking glass on top. Branch introduced Gail to the lawmen in his past as Gail introduced him to her sister Cindy and husband Carl as well as her best friend from her college year. Just before dinner was announced, Branch and Gail approached Captain Ennis and his wife.

"We are glad you're here from so far away, and I presume you got my letter." "Yes, and like previous marshals and bounty hunters before you such as Swanson, Harnel, Adams and McWain; it's just a matter of time before you resign your lawman status. But until then, I hope you and Gail will continue to be available to PF and Pappy for special situations. I will be looking for your permanent replacement ASAP. I understand that a thriving business and a family is trumping the assets of a lawman's way of life with its daily life-threatening situations. Of course, a beautiful wife only makes the transition so much easier, heh?"

Their discussion was cut short by Sylvia smacking a large spoon on an empty pot. "Dinner is served, we have two meals, a choice of carved roast beef by the chef, or chicken pot pie. Both include homemade buttered rolls, baked potatoes or home-fries, choice of carrots, turnip or peas. Serve yourselves to coffee or tea and later we will serve a choice of several desserts."

After sitting down and responding to the traditional ringing of spoons against glasses, the Duo was finally able to talk to each other. "Guess we are now married; do you remember much of the minister's words?" Gail said, "I only heard you say, 'I do." "Well so did I, but I knew that the 'die was cast' when the minister said, 'you may now kiss your bride.' Are you happy?" "Very much so, and pleased not to continue carrying on a surreptitious love affair. Now I can have an open love affair with my husband, heh?' "For sure."

The meal was a total success and more visiting continued throughout the afternoon. At 5PM PF showed up with a buggy and the newlywed's luggage. Branch decided to make a short speech to thank the guests for their attendance. Gail whispered, "now don't start prattling, and make it short. The train to Dallas is waiting and my body needs to be cooled down, right!" "Yes Ma'am. Will do on both counts."

After expressing their thanks, the Duo stopped at the marshal's office to change into comfortable traveling clothes, and boarded the train for a three-hour trip to the Princess Hotel in the center of Dallas.

*

The trip provided some time to catch a nap. It soon became dark and the swaying of the passenger car, along with the clickety-clack of the wheels over the railing joints was conducive to a restful ride. Arriving at the hotel by 10PM, the newlyweds made it to their room. There the ritual of tender love making started. Their familiarity with intimacy made it easier to proceed to consummating their marriage. Once they copulated, Gail responded immediately with prolonged spasms that induced her lover to their mutual nirvana.

After expending their lust, Gail said, "I guess, I waited all my life for this moment. Now that it has passed, it is not simply ended, it is the beginning of a life-long love making with each other." "Yes, and I will always try to make it a special event."

And a special event it was, for no one got any sleep that night. After several welcomed couplings, the Duo finally called on room service for their first replenishing breakfast—breakfast in bed. Throughout the day, they talked, made love, ate their meals and after two days, they finally dressed and went walking downtown.

The stores were divided into very specific wares. There did not seem to have any local general mercantiles. When inquired, they were told that the specific stores in the neighborhood were called boutiques and in the center of town were located the new department stores that held everything from clothing to furniture and hardware. Taking a taxi into the center of the city, they experienced the coldness of shopping without the fine touch of an attendant. Gail said, "yes, they do have everything, and if they don't have it, you don't need it."

They spent the rest of their week enjoying the fine restaurants and theaters. One evening at supper Branch asked, "is theater spelled theater or theatre?" Gail said, "either one is correct, but in America we use theater, and the rest of the world uses theatre." That same night after some tender love making Gail said, "I don't think I'm ever gonna get enough of you, and it don't matter if we are in this magnificent hotel or in the barn of our ranch. I think it is time to go back to Waco, for that is our future, don't you agree?" "Let's pack up and we'll take the first train to Waco come morning. I agree with you, I just didn't want to be the one to put an end to our honeymoon." "If I have anything to do about this, we'll never end our honeymoon—we'll live it day by day. Now make love to me!"

The next morning, the Duo sent a telegram to his parents, asking them to meet them with a buggy at the train depot by 1PM. Their ride to home was a pleasant time. They started talking how they would divide their work hours and who would "own" which part of the business. Branch suggested that he be in charge of the racing division and marketing of their crops. Gail would manage the work and riding horses from afar. She made it clear that she was not a horse handler but that she inherited the business management abilities from Otis. She also wanted total involvement in the accounting of the crops, along with the overall accounting of riding, work, and racing horses.

Branch thought about it and finally said, "so, you're going to be our full time working financial officer, and I'm going to get to do what I want with racing horses and crops?" "Yes, absolutely. As long as both divisions make money to support the entire ranch." "So what happens if my two divisions lose money one year?" "Then the remainder of the ranch will support your divisions. That's what marriage is all about, heh?"

Arriving at the Waco train depot, the senior Wests were waiting for the Duo. After hugs and kisses, Alden and Flora were happy to greet their new daughter-in-law. When Branch went to load his luggage in the buggy, there was already luggage in the allotted space. "Where are you guys going?" "Home. Let's have dinner at Sylvia's and we'll explain."

Alden started, "you were smart to have us stay in your ranch house and have our meals at the cook shack. This is a beautiful ranch, winters are mild compared to Durango, you have incredible people working for you, and mom has already made friends with Annette and Jane. I'm very interested in working with crops, and If your offer still stands, we would love to return and join you." Gail added, "and I would get the mother I lost years ago. Welcome home mom!"

Alden added, "we are staying in the railroad hotel tonight, taking the train back to Durango tomorrow, arrange to officially retire, sell the house, and pack our belongings and furniture. In a month, or whenever the house is built, we'll be back."

And so the Duo was ready to take on the business and grow it to match current times.

***

CHAPTER 11

Ranching, Racing & Harvesting

The next morning, talking over their replenishing breakfast, Gail said, "I have a dozen letters and or telegrams from the old suppliers of our work horses. I will either answer their letters or respond with a telegram. So I'll be going to town today." "But you are not going alone. I will see Gary and find out who would qualify as your bodyguard. For today and whenever the business takes you off this ranch—and this is not negotiable." "So be it, I won't fight you on this. So what are you doing today?" "I'm jumping into the realm of horse racing and I'll tell you more later. I'm certain that things moved along during our honeymoon. So today will be catchup day."

Meeting with Gary, "Is there a worker that we can trust to serve as Gail's bodyguard when she is off the ranch?" "Yes and I have the man for you. Wes Stubridge, aka Stu, is a 55-year-old cowboy in charge of the cattle. He is a real 'jack of all trades' on this ranch and is the best man with a handgun and pump-shotgun. Most importantly, he has sand!"

"This man would have to work on the premises, and not go out in the field." "Stu could be our float and could help anyone who would need help." "Is he in the field, cause I'd like to speak with him." "He was kept back so I could talk with him. He has already agreed that a change in workload would be welcomed." "Fine, let's go see him."

After pleasantries were finished Branch got to the point with two questions. First, "as my wife's bodyguard, are you ready to take a bullet for her." "Without a doubt, anyone who wants a piece of her will have to take me out and I don't go down easy."

"Second, Gail don't know it yet, but she's going to need an assistant who knows everything about this ranch; as well as help out when Gary has someone who needs help as long as you stay away from the field." "It would be my pleasure to follow Gail about and Gary knows I would help out anytime." "Great, from now on, you wear your Colt at all times. When you go into town, bring your 1893 pump-shotgun." "Agreed."

Branch then went to look for Toby. The new barn was coming along. The racing horse section was completed with four large 12X14 free housing stalls, a half dozen standard 6 foot wide tethered horse stalls, and a large tack room which included an office for Gary. The carpenters were finishing the other general use stalls and tack room. Branch liked what he saw and was then directed to the racetrack under construction.

Toby was busy riding the back-blade scraper as the cropboys were manning the disc, finish harrows, and packing roller. Toby came over to Branch and said, "things are moving along, the racehorses will be moved to their new quarters in a few days once the banging and sawing is done. The racetrack will be ready tomorrow. The red dirt has enough clay to be compactable thereby providing good traction for racing. I'm also making a turnaround at the ¼ mile to train the horses to make a controlled turn around a post, and race the last ¼ mile—that's the new standard coming at the major racetracks."

"How is Randy Martin working out?" "Fantastic, a great kid and a natural racer. He came yesterday with his parents to watch him race the horses on the main road. Boy, was I glad to see that his parents were small people that didn't reach 5 feet. That's a good sign for our jockey. Despite all this, there will be a problem." "And that is?" "Our six racehorses need to be exercised at least twice a day for 45 minutes each time. This should be done by someone not weighing more than 70 pounds, since we are trying to hold Randy's weight at 60-70 pounds." "Wow, that's a full-time job and it's going to be a problem to find someone with that weight limit, why even your slim wife must weigh at least a hundred pounds?"

"Uh-uh, not necessarily, turn around and look at a good candidate. Branch turned around and saw no one. "Hello Mister West, my name is Winn Stevens, I'm good with horses, a good rider and will be a reliable worker." Branch kept looking about but finally felt someone pulling on his britches. Branch looked down and saw a 'little man.' "Hell, you're a midget—well, doing a classic hip-slapper, blow me over. You're hired."

*

The weeks went by, the hay was growing, more land was being cultivated, and Gail was busy making arrangements to bring her purchases of young geldings, draft horses as well as young and mature mares. The new ranch racing section was taking shape. Every night and both weekend days were spent racing the horses at both the ¼ and ½ mile distances. Toby had named all six of his racehorses—two colts and four fillies. The three purchased at the AA ranch were: Wildfire, Lady and Blondie. The three horses selected out of the general population were: Sidewinder, Belle, and Red.

The day Gary and Branch clocked Wildfire and Lady do the ¼ mile in 19 seconds, they knew those two were ready to race. Sidewinder was also close at 22 seconds, but he looked funny walking sideways. At the races, he would be laughed at, but Branch realized that he would serve as a deceptive Trojan Horse to bidders.

For their first race, Branch would walk Wildfire himself into town the next Saturday. After registration, including a $250 entrance fee, Branch registered Randy Martin as the racing jockey. The only racing rule was that a horse could only advance to the next race if he won the last race—competing one on one. Since there were only six entries, by the unlucky card draw, Wildfire would have to win two races to get to the final race. A bit archaic system, but it was the traditional way things were done in town. Each horse was given a different colored towel to attach to the saddle's cantle. That way betting was done each race by the color of the horse's towel—Wildfire was red.

After registration, betting people would walk about the six horses. Wildfire was a newcomer with a kid on its back. Branch thought that was not impressive, but when the odds were established by the house, Wildfire was given 1:6 odds. The favorite horse who had won in the past was given a 1:2 odds and was ridden by an obvious favorite cowboy.

The entire ranch workers and cropboys were present, and each worker placed their own bets from $1 to $10, except for Stu who dropped the maximum bet of $200 as directed by Gail. The racers were called to the starting line. Wildfire was wild from the crowd's hooting and hollering. Randy was seen flipping up the eye blinders and talking in Wildfire's ears. The horse responded and went still with flexed hind muscles. At the sound of gunfire, Wildfire bolted like a bullet and left the competitor a full length behind at the ¼ mile marker. The ranch's $200 bet yielded $1,200 and Randy earned his first $100.

The odds for the second race changed. The three remaining horses had each won their first race. Wildfire had to race one of these horses and then the other, assuming he won this second race. The odds were set at 1:4 for Wildfire and

1:8 for the competitor. The bank was gambling that Wildfire would win again and all the competitor's bets would be profit for the bank. Toby whispered to Branch, "are they up for a surprise, some of those half-wits should realize that a stallion is just getting primed for the next race." Gail gave Stu the nod and he placed another $300 on Wildfire—the red horse.

Just as the race was setting up, an elderly well-dressed gentleman in the crowd noticed Randy whisper to Wildfire as he flipped the blinders. Wildfire again settled down and pulled back his hind quarters like the hammer was pulled back on a Colt. On the gunshot, the race was again done in 20 seconds and Wildfire was ahead by half a length. With 1:4 odds, Wildfire had earned another $1,200 and Randy another $50.

With a half hour break before the finale, a stately man came up and said to Branch, "I'll give you $5,000 for that horse and saddle." "No thanks, we've been training a long-term racehorse, and he's not for sale." "$10,000." "I know, that a bird in hand is worth more than a hundred on the fly, but I'm willing to gamble my chances on this horse."

The last race as a half mile total distance consisted of two ¼ mile sprints separated by a turning post at ¼ mile. Randy says, "the key to winning this race is a good tight turn at the post. The greater the arc, the greater the lost time to catch up. So based on these facts, whichever horse starts on the left has the advantage to do a left turn at the post and the other horse is doomed to the wider arc." "How is the position chosen?" "Coin toss—heads or tails."

Now the competing horse is a longer distance racer and has won this race frequently. So we have two winners and how the bank sets the odds will be a surprise especially since they made a bundle on the last race.

Awaiting the odds, the competing rider was making sly remarks about the Wildfire's wimpy saddle, eye blinkers, a hackamore bridle without a mouth bit, and using a kid to ride a man's mount. Toby was listening to all this and walked up to motor-mouth and said, "you can laugh all you want but you'd better be on your best game.

Also, I see that you are using a whipping quirt, so make sure you quirt your horse and not ours or our jockey—we'll be watching you."

The odds came out Wildfire 1:4 and motor-mouth's mount 1:8 with a maximum bid of $500. Branch said to Toby, Gail and Gary, "they are still banking on Wildfire winning and they'll make a fortune out of the losses with the competitor." "So be it, let's bet on our own horse and make some money. Jane came up and said she still had $100 from wedding presents and placed it on the red horse at 1:4 odds. Stu went up and placed $500 on the ranch's behalf, and added a second bet of $100. Branch was watching and saw their workers all drop $50-100 on Wildfire.

Tensions were high and Wildfire relished the energy. At a toss of the coin, Randy said heads and tails ended up. Randy then set Wildfire on the right-hand side and knew he had to get a full length ahead before the turning post if he was to gain position. With both horses lined up, the motor-mouth repeated the same line, "now don't fall during the turn, boy!" Randy did his usual flipping up the blinders, whisper in his ears and felt the horse's hind quarters cock up.

On the gunshot, both horses bolted up, Randy was playing the reins to edge Wildfire while motor-mouth was viciously quirting his horse. Despite the horse abuse, Wildfire got ahead a full length before the turning post and did a perfect turn. Motor-mouth was so irritated that he whipped the quirt onto Randy's back and the crowd booed in response. The race continued and Wildfire came in with two lengths to spare. The crowd roared and the officials came up to the riders. "Mister Sledgehead, you are disqualified for abusing your horse and battery on the opposing jockey. You are also banned from this racetrack for the next two years. Young man, congratulations on a great race and for not faltering when you were whipped."

The Duo left with $4,000, and all the workers left with $200-600 in their pockets. Branch then told Gail, "our next race will be at McGalloway's in Dallas." "Why not closer, like in town." "Because, our winning horse is now marked, as well as all our other racers in our barn. We'll never get winning odds here after today. In Dallas, we'll just be a newbie in town with just another Quarter horse. Except that we'll be there with as many horses as Toby says are ready and we'll include our Trojan Horse—they'll laugh at him, but not for long, hey?"

*

Getting back to the daily routine, Gail had heard Ansel tell his stories how Jane had a knack and talent in teaching the work horses. Weeks ago, at Jane's first day at work, Ansel had given Jane her first task—a strong willed gelding that refused to learn basic commands. Jane took the task and applied her own routine. Talking, touching, rubbing, brushing softly, and then walking away. Returning in 10 minutes with a sugar cube and repeating her routine. Finally adding one basic command, "go ahead/ stop." Repeating it over and over again, then adding gee and haw. The day continued with Jane suddenly walking away, but returning with a treat—even if it was just a handful of oats to be eaten out of her hand.

During the noon dinner break, the gelding was seen waiting at the pasture's gate. As soon as he saw her, he neighed loudly till Jane escorted him to the training room. By 4PM, Jane went to get Ansel to give him a show. The gelding performed the ten basic commands, but then Jane added: step aside, back up, lift up foot and move over the wagon's tongue, go away when crowding worker in a stall, and stand and wait. When the demo was done, Jane said, "that's a good boy." To Ansel's shock, the horse nodded his head up and down in agreement.

Meanwhile, knowing that Ansel had Jane's help, Gail had been actively looking for two-year-old geldings and mares as well as mature mares for breeding. These were all horses from neighboring ranchers that had no or little training. Most cattle ranchers did not have the time to train horses and continue feeding them till they could be functionally used. For this reason, Gail was able to purchase all the young horses she wanted at a discount—as long as they were Quarter horses and Belgian drafts as sorrels, chestnuts or bays.

The influx of about a hundred extra horses in need of training in saddle riding, cow punching, and harnessing simply overwhelmed all the workers who dealt in training. After hearing of the worries, Gail and Branch addressed the problem. After breakfast, Gail went first, "so to help with the overload, does anyone have a suggestion?" Things went dead quiet and to everyone's surprise it was Oscar of all people who stood up and said, "every day I do the chores that Uncle Zeke gives me, and I always have 2 free hours before supper. I can help train any of these horses if you allow me!"

Ansel stood up and said, "Oscar, you can work with me anytime and I appreciate your offer. How about starting today?" "Obediah got up and said, how about helping me out with horses that need to be prepared for a saddle?" Winn, the midget, got up and said, "with school being out, Randy is available every day to exercise the horses. I am free and I know I can help with training." Stu, the bodyguard, was next to get up, "I have a lot of free time, and I'll help too." Toby got up and said, "I'll make the time and help you all as well." Gail looked at the four trainers, Obediah, Benny, Ansel, and Jane and got a firm nod of approval.

Branch got up and said, "we can hire more help if no one is interested in overtime work after supper?" The cook shack exploded in hollers, whistles, and guffaws. "I guess you are all interested, heh? So, since you're all on salary, we'll pay $2 for two hours work any evening. If any of you want to work Sunday afternoon, we'll pay $5 from 1PM to suppertime. This we have to schedule, so for those interested please see Gail. We'll continue this till the harvest starts when all hands will be on deck. But during the harvest, there will also be overtime pay for anyone who is willing to work beyond five 8-hour days."

For the next 10 days, there was a hustle and bustle as every worker was involved in training. All evenings and Sundays were booked up full. By the time the harvest started everyone was in a good mood with extra cash in their pockets—but no time to go to town to spend it since hay was arriving at the baling station.

*

During those ten days, Branch concentrated on the land cultivation and the preparation for the harvest. Gary was busy with both activities as Gail was supervising the push to train the new horses. Branch asked Gary, "how many acres can a team of horses plow in one day?" "Historically with a single blade plow and a team of large geldings, we could turn over one acre in four hours with one rest/watering period. After lunch we would change teams and repeat the process for the next four hours—for a total of 2 acres per day. Today, we use the new double-bladed plow pulled by a team of Belgian drafts. We change teams after dinner and by supper time we have four plowed acres. The team of geldings match the draft horses and do the disc and finish harrows."

"In summary to produce four finished acres per day, it takes 4 draft horses on the plow, four geldings on the disc harrows, and four geldings on the finish harrows." "I see, and in a month's time we have 100 acres ready to seed." "Yes and to be up to date, we have 200 acres of mature but early hay, 50 acres of land ready for seeding oats after the first crop's harvest, and we have 100 acres to be seeded late this summer to get hay started before the dormant winter. Now, if you want to expand beyond 350 acres, let me know after the fall oats harvest." "So you are planning 300 acres of hay and 50 acres of oats yearly, and the 50 oat's acres will be rotated every six years by cultivating 50 acres of the hay fields every year?" "Yes and heavily fertilizing with manure." "Fine, sounds like a good plan for now, let's see how the 200-acre harvest goes and how the market will bear to handle our surplus."

Gary needed to bring up the subject of marketing. "Now that you said the word surplus, let's talk about the surplus we will have this year. Last year, we fed 100 tons of hay and 25 tons of straw. The neighbors bought all our surplus of another 100 tons of hay and 25 tons of oats. But this year we will have another 200 tons of surplus to dispose of. How do you plan to market all this hay?" "I'll find some distributors in Dallas or Austin or both." "Great, now both these areas are 100 miles away, how do you plan to get your product there?" "By a railroad spur to my hay shed." "Hu'um, do you know someone or something that I don't know?" "Maybe, we'll talk again, for sure!"

"Moving on, how are we set up for division of forces when the harvest starts?" "The cropboys will handle getting the hay to the baling platform and help unload it. That will include two mowers from dawn to dusk, one tedder/side/finish rake, one on the loader, two men stacking hay and two men exchanging wagons to and from the balers. That will include four full time cropboys and four repeating seasonal workers."

"So the finishing portion is the baling and disposal of the 50-pound bales." "Yes, the local ranchers will arrive with altered wagons that will hold a ton of hay, or 40 bales. Gail will collect the 75 cents a bale or $30 a ton. Once the ranchers are all loaded up, the balance of the bales are moved by conveyor belt to the hay shed."

"I have divided the 200 acres into 10 acre working plots—equal to 20 plots. Since we have agreed to three crops by starting the first crop early, I will predict that we will harvest 5 tons each day's 10-acre plot. That 5 tons works out to be +- 200 bales a day. Since a baler can put out 10 bales an hour, our two balers will put out 20 bales an hour or take +- 10 hours to do the job which comes to a 10-hour shift for 20 days to cover all 20-ten-acre plots."

"That's pretty fancy ciphering, so how many workers do we need to put out 20 bales an hour?" "One to unload the hay wagons, two to feed the baler, two to apply the twine, one to move the bales to the ranchers or the conveyor belt, and a horse to walk in circles all day without any man herding him. An extra man is needed to stack the conveyed bales in the shed. Plus, a relief supervisor for each baler."

"And who may I ask are the supervisors?" "Why, you and me, of course!" "For sure, don't you think I need to learn each job by doing each job before I become a supervisor? "No time, you'll have to multitask, heh?" "For sure."

"I see you have hired seasonal workers to help the cropboys, have you hired any help to cover both balers for a total of 10 hours a day." "Yes, we will have 8 extra men and several on the waiting list if we need them. The ladies are all busy, Gail is counting and cashing in the ranchers and peeling potatoes on the off time, Jane is the water gal for the field workers and horses, and Annette is a parttime worker on the baling platform and the parttime cook's helper along with Gail."

"And amidst all this, there is a carpenter crew building our second bunkhouse and one crew starting to build my parent's house and barn." "Yes, it's going to be a push till the oats are harvested and winter starts." Branch thought, *"in-between all this activity, I have to send a telegram to Walter Litchfield, arrange for a rail spur to be added, find a hay/straw distributor in Dallas or Austin, or both, enter a big mid-summer horserace in Dallas and keep my new wife happy."*

Before anyone knew it, the harvest started. On day three, the first load of loose hay arrived at 9AM. Two men applied a three-prong hook tied to a rope over a pulley and gantry. A resting horse pulled half the load of hay off and moved it on the gantry and dropped it on the concrete platform. The second hookup emptied the load. Then two workers started feeding the hopper with three prong hay forks. The horse was walking in circles while turning the cam that converted the energy to the baler's plunger and knives. Branch was learning to feed the twine and tie a non- slip knot. In the first hour, he learned every job and then would relieve workers when someone had to use the privy or needed a rest. They had a regular water break for all every 90 minutes, plus anytime a worker needed extra water. Gail had prepared a tasty drink which consisted of ginger, salt, and sugar in a gallon of water. The advantage over water was enhanced hydration and energy boosting.

Everyone had a half hour for the noon dinner, and only one baler's staff could go at a time. The field workers also split their staff for the dinner break. That way, the system continued, at a slower pace, but easy to resume full production.

The workers were in good spirits and making some extra cash. The seasonal workers were well fed and well paid and many were returning help. The ranchers kept coming at full force and finally Branch asked what the push was to buy hay reserves. The old timers clearly said that a drought was coming, and now was the time to build an inventory to save their herds.

After a week's work on the baling platform, Branch said, "the old timers are saying we're heading for a drought this summer and it will last till next spring. Let's say it does happen to occur, how can we save our second and third hay crops and our one oats crop?" "My dad and uncle had always said that the river to our north is on high ground and our pastures and hay fields are all downhill. They said that trenching off the river could easily flood our land and could be controlled by damming up the trenches for selected releases." "Boy, old timers knew how to use nature, and we are moving away towards modernization—a sign of the times."

The harvest continued for the next two weeks. It was clear that if the crop fields kept expanding, that a third baler and mower would be needed as minimal additions to keep up the 20-day schedule of harvesting the first crop of 300 hay acres instead of the present 200. The early harvest was better than expected and 180 tons of quality hay was baled. The ranchers took half and held back to get some second and third crop which had more leaves than stems and had higher nutrition value.

Once all overtime pay and wages were doled out, the Duo decided to have an 'end of project meeting.' Zeke expressed a universal feeling. "We are all glad to help out during the harvest and we certainly appreciate the extra cash but there is a problem. The horse maintenance and training staff cannot afford to take 3 weeks off four times during the summer—that's for three hay crops and one oats crop. We are already three weeks behind and we don't think you will accept the unfavorable business delays. So, the silent majority who have asked me to fall on my sword are anxiously awaiting your response."

The Duo looked at each other and Gail, getting the nod, said, "well- spoken Zeke.

Branch and I agree, and, in the future, we will hire the seasonal help necessary. If we have a second shift, we can still offer you regulars the opportunity of working an occasional 2nd shift and make the extra cash." The applause, chortles and whistles were proof that the crowd was in full acceptance.

Afterwards Branch brought out the subject of drought. The need for irrigation was explained. Gary would undertake the construction of trenches, dams, and release gates along the river to the north. The crop boys would be the workers to accomplish this within a week so the harvested 200 acres could be irrigated asap.

In a week's time, the ranch was invited to Dallas for the first big horse race of the summer. The 100-mile trip cost $6 for a round trip ticket to be used the same day. The ranch would pay the ticket fee as a measure of gratitude for the harvest going so smoothly. Now, Branch, Toby, Randy, Winn and even Stu were getting a team of race ready horses prepared for the coming races.

Five days later Branch asked how things were going. "Winn and Randy did a fine job exercising and racing the horses according to my schedule. I guarantee you that they did not lose any ground. Actually, they are more ready now than ever. I suggest that we bring four horses, but race only three of them in the three different races." The three racers were Wildfire, Lady, Sidewinder and Belle as backup. All four horses were proven to do the ¼ mile in 21 seconds or better. As in big races, the horses were encouraged to arrive the day before the race and spend the night in the race stable's comfort stalls. Stu and Winn escorted the four horses to Dallas along with their best hay and oats grain. To guarantee security, both men slept in the stables with their horses.

The next day, the Duo arrived with all their workers. The morning was dedicated to qualifying the horses. Each horse was clocked individually on the ¼ mile sprint. Since no one knew what the best scores for qualifying would be acceptable, every horse was pushed to its max ability. Toby was writing the times for each horse and after the qualifying informed the Duo. "They are taking only the top eight horses for three races—a team of four to race the ½ mile track, a team of two for the ¼ mile race and a team of two for the finale ½ mile track. I have listed every horse's time and we need to wait for the official announcement."

One hour later the eight racehorses were announced along with the betting odds. Lady (#6) made it to the four-horse team ½ mile race, Sidewinder (#3) got the second race ¼ mile race, and Wildfire (#7) got the finale ½ mile race. The odds table was then posted and to everyone's surprise included odds for first and second place:

RACE ONE (to win or place second)
    #1 1:2 win 1:2 for second
    #2 1:4 win 1:3 for second
    #4 1:6 win 1:5 for second
    #6 1:8 win 1:6 for second (LADY)
RACE TWO (to win or place second)
    #8 1:2 win 1:2 for second
    #3 1:8 win 1:6 for second (SIDEWINDER)

RACE THREE (to win or place second)
  #5 1:2 win 1:2 for second
  #7 1: 8 win 1:6 for second (WILDFIRE)

Branch then had to pay the three entrance fees totaling $750. Then Toby started playing the odds of the documented times of each horse and finally said, with all the Circle W workers lending an ear, the maximum bet is $500. Put your money as follows: In Race One, place the max bet on Lady 1:6 to come in SECOND PLACE. In Race Two, place the max bet on Sidewinder 1:6 to come in SECOND PLACE. In Race Three, place the max bet on Wildfire 1:8 to WIN. And if I'm wrong, Jane and I will move out of town." Randy and Winn were not allowed to know these betting odds. That guaranteed that the jockeys would do their best to win the race and not appear to throw the race to make money.

Before the race, the eight racehorses were paraded before the grandstand. Winn was riding Sidewinder who was prancing sideways, and everyone laughed at the midget on a crazy horse. Jane was on Lady, but Randy would be racing Lady and Wildfire, as Winn would race Sidewinder. Once the bets were entered for Race One, the horses were called to the starting line. Randy could tell that Lady was tense, so he whispered in her ear till she settled down. The card draw had placed Lady onto position 2, just right of position 1, which was the second-best place for a left hand turn. Just before the gunshot, Randy flipped the binders, lifted his body off the saddle and could feel Lady's back arch in readiness.

As the horses took off, Randy was taken back at the roar four horses made, compounded by the horror of four horses heading for the same turn at an estimated 50 mph. Fortunately the horse on Lady's left made a tight turn next to the post and Lady tried to cut in front but the horse was too fast and kept the lead to the finish line. Randy was at a total loss when he saw all the Circle W workers jump up hollering like a bunch of fools. Randy's pa was present and explained the betting odds, but clarified that

Randy would have to win Race Three for the workers to win.

The second race was Winn's first race. Winn's small appearance was exaggerated when sitting on a full-size Quarter Horse. But once he stood up on his stirrups, everyone realized that he was truly a contender and properly matched as a jockey. No one was laughing now.

With both horses at the ready, the gunshot rang off. The bystanders were amazed at the strength of both horses and the intent of both jockeys to encourage their mount to push harder. At the finish line, it was good that there were three judges standing on an elevated platform. The two horses came in withing a nose and horse #8 was declared the winner by a vote of 2 to 1, thus pushing Sidewinder into second place. Winn was somewhat shocked to see his coworkers coming at him, thinking he was going to get an ear full. Instead, Zeke grabbed Winn, placed him on his shoulders, and paraded him about the finish line like a king. The Duo later explained to Winn the significance of coming in second when all his coworkers were betting on this outcome. It was Gail who said that future races would be handled differently, since the jockeys always needed to be free of influence from odds and actual betting.

The last race was about to start, and Wildfire was wild about the hooting crowd. Toby noted that the opponent's jockey was an older man and was certainly a professional racer. The horse's owner looked mighty familiar to Branch, but he couldn't place him to an event or place in the past. Branch did note the horse's brand, the "Bar S." His trying to recall the face came to an end as the race was ready to begin. The toss of the coin placed Wildfire to the right of horse #5—again at a disadvantage at a left-hand turn.

At the gunshot, the crowd came alive. Despite the tight turn made by horse #5, once the turn was made, both horses were seen nose to nose heading down the main stretch. It was clear that #5 was not as strong as Wildfire and his jockey knew it. So, the jockey was whipping #5 wildly with a short quirt. Despite this, Wildfire gained an entire horse length and won the race. Again, the Circle W workers were excessively jubilant. The three judges came to the Duo and said, "you have some fantastic horses and when you return, best to expect different odds and we won't ever use second place odds ever again. We'll be going back to 'winner take all' and have more races to compensate for the losses."

The train back to Waco left at 7PM. So being only 4PM, most of the workers hit the saloons for drinks and celebration. The Wests, Irvings, and Ashburns got together and met at a busy diner for supper. The three couples added their winnings. The Ashburns made $2,100, the Irvings made $1,200 and the Wests made $10,000 minus their $500 bets, $750 in registration fees and $200 in jockey fees. Randy had made $50 for Race One, and $100 for Race Three. Winn had made $50 for Race Two and couldn't believe he made so much money for losing a race.

Putting their money aside, the three couples were happy to have all the workers on the train to help protect their winnings. After a great supper of prime rib with a vegetable casserole, the three couples started talking about what was ahead. Gary started, "my hands are full with this irrigation project and starting to cultivate another 100 acres." Toby was next to say, "my plate is full. The next race is in Austin sometime between the second and third crop. We hope to enter all six races with our six horses—assuming that all six racehorses qualify. There's a lot of training involved, and we can get it done—thanks to Randy and Winn. Annette added, "Gary wants me to advertise for more seasonal crop workers and help with the interviews. Zeb is working me full time especially with the added garden and so many extra workers to feed. Jane was last to say, "and don't wonder what I'll be doing with these extra 100 horses we have to train." Gail was curious and asked, "are either of you ladies being overworked by Ansel, Benny, Obadiah or Zeb?" Both ladies answered at the same time, "absolutely not. Our working conditions are the best any woman could ever expect. We have no complaints."

The Duo then took their turns. Branch said that he and Gail would take a trip to Dallas and Austin to find hay distributors and feed stores to handle their commercial enterprise. Branch would also be working on getting a rail spur to his hay shed and Gail would begin a new endeavor.

***

CHAPTER 12

Commercialization

The days following the Dallas race were unbearable days with temperatures of 100+ degrees in full sun. The cropboys were busy irrigating the crop fields and pastures. By flooding some 500 acres every other day the harvested acres had shown green regrowth and the pastures had maintained green grass. Since the river was so large, no effect on the water's total volume was ever detected.

Now ten days into the drought, it was clear that central Texas was burning up. The Duo went to see the agricultural agent in town and he informed them that the entire 200 miles of central Texas between Waco, thru Austin and to San Antonio, were going to suffer a drought this summer, and no one knew how long it would last. Yet north to Dallas and south to the Rio Grande Valley would be spared ground.

With this information, the Duo decided to head out to Austin and find a hay distributor. When Branch went to the railroad ticket office to schedule their trip, he happened to ask the agent, "is there a man, by the name of Walter Litchfield, who might work for this railroad?" The agent said, "let me look up the name in the yearly directory." After a few minutes, the agent looked above his glasses and said, "sir, Mister Litchfield is the new manager of the line between Waco and San Antonio and he is stationed in Austin." "Well isn't that a stroke of serendipity; I'll take two tickets to Austin and please send Mister Litchfield this telegram."

To: Walter Litchfield
From: Branch West

A ghost from Lajunta past STOP
Do you remember shooting a robber in the knee STOP

I need a railway spur to my crop enterprise STOP

On way to Austin in three days STOP

May we have a meeting with you STOP

The next day Randy showed up with a telegram from Austin railroad headquarters— from Walter Litchfield. Gail read the telegram:

Remember that day like it was yesterday STOP

Still carry that mini pistol STOP

Can still see conductor slip in blood and land on butt STOP

Looking forward to our meeting STOP

Platform agent will escort you to my office STOP

Three days later, the Duo boarded the train to Austin with personal luggage for several days and a carpetbag full of this year's first crop hay. The hay's aroma, being freshly harvested, whiffed thru the carpetbag's cloth enclosure. Branch started sniffing the air and several of the passengers followed suit. Gail finally said, "you trickster, you've got all the passengers wondering who works in a barn!" "Yup, now watch the conductor who is coming in to punch our tickets. Once he gets a whiff, he is going to look at everyone's boots to see who is covered in manure, heh?" "And the first thing he's going to do is open some windows, for sure!"

With the windows open, the barn smell disappeared. To pass the time Gail said, "if we are really going to have a drought, is there anything we can quickly plant to add to our products?" "If the cropboys started plowing another plot right away, either 50 or 100 acres, we could plant another crop of oats. The straw is sellable at half the hay price, but the oats grain will go at a premium in a drought." "Well, don't you think we should consider doing just that. We certainly have eight full time cropboys; and we can hire seasonal workers to open the irrigation gates."

"I guess we've been living together long enough, since we are beginning to think alike. I was planning to discuss this with you, but I did ask Gary to start cultivating a new plot of land while we were gone, and we would discuss it again upon our return." "Why of course, we think alike. I never have to ask you for intimate relations, and you seem to know when I'm in the mood?" "That's an easy one, you're always in the mood every morning and night. Duuhhhhh." Gail was going to add a retort, but noticed that some of the passengers were listening too intently, so instead she cautiously passed her hand over Branch's crotch and brought a cautious smile to his face.

Arriving in Austin, as soon as the Duo stepped on the platform, two men grabbed their luggage and one man escorted them to a RR carriage. After a short ride, the Duo was escorted to the third floor and were seated in the waiting room of Director Litchfield's private office. A secretary came to greet them with cold glasses of lemonade and said that the Director was finishing a meeting and would be with them in minutes. Shortly, Walter Litchfield popped thru the door and extended his hand to greet Branch. "Nice to see you again, and you still look awful young. Now who is this lovely lady?" "This is my wife Gail." After all introductions and pleasantries, including reliving the event on the train, the Director said, "now tell me about your business and why you need a rail spur."

Branch and Gail went thru the full description of the horses, land, buildings and special attention to the crop business. Branch than added, "we have 200 acres of hay, 100 acres of oats and will be adding another 100 acres of hay next year. This year we are planning on harvesting 600+ tons in three hay crops and one oats crop. We will use 100+ tons for our ranch, sell 100 tons to neighbors and have 400+ tons for sale to a distributor in Austin. That amounts to 25 tons per box car, or a total of 16 boxcars this year and a significant increase next year." Gail added, "without a spur on our ranch, we will have to haul all this hay to the rail yard—making it totally unfeasible."

"I see, any idea how far you are from the main trunk line heading southwest from Waco?" "Yes, I walked it with my foreman with a 100-yard tape and we came to +-1/4 mile. We'll also need a switch on the main trunk line that makes a wide ramp heading to our ranch, a road crossing for wagons on the local traveling road, and a double rail with a simple switch that holds three boxcars each next to my hay shed."

"Amazing, it's so nice to see someone who knows what they want. Well you are correct, when I heard what you needed, I sent the Waco engineer to scout and prepare a construction estimate—and he agrees 100% with your assessment."

Gail then said, "Assuming it is feasible, what will this cost us," as she pulls her bank book out of her reticule. "Today, now 25 years since completion of the Transcontinental Railroad, we still charge $16,000 a mile as long as we don't have to build trestles, dig out tunnels or blast thru rock. So ¼ mile will cost you $4,000, the wide switch is $500, the road crossing is $250, and the simple switch at the ranch is $250. For a total of $5,000 you'll have your functional spur in three weeks." "Branch adds, "that's great, that means we'll have it for the second crop." Getting the nod, Gail starts to write a bank draft.

"Gail, hold off on writing a bank draft, I have a story to tell. After the attempted train robbery and saving my life, I invited Branch to my private car. After refreshments and some pleasant conversation, I asked him how much I owed him for grateful services rendered. Do you have any idea what he said?" "Yes, and he was right to refuse a reward." "Yes, he did say that I owed him nothing. However, before I invited him to my car, I had already written a bank draft for $10,000—the usual and customary 10% recovery fee for $100,000. As a matter of fact, this is the bank draft dated last year that I kept in my safe. So, today, I'll replace this old $10,000 bank draft with this current one for $5,000 and your rail spur is now paid in full. My engineer will start laying track tomorrow. And if you recall Branch, I did say that we would meet again, and make things right!" "Yes you did and thank you."

Before leaving the RR office, the Duo informed themselves as to who used train freight service to distribute hay and feed. The name Hofstetter Distributors came up, with an address next to the railroad yard. The Duo decided to find a diner for dinner before visiting the hay distributor in the afternoon. Sitting down at Georgie's Place, the Duo ordered an all-American meal of meatloaf, mashed potatoes, tomato sauce on the side, and peas with fresh baked buttered bread. Waiting for their food, Branch asked what she had in mind for this secret project that she hinted at." Gail smiled and said, "I knew that your curiosity would come to a boil, I'm just surprised that it took this long."

"Well, I couldn't come up with the answer until this morning. Since we are here making a business deal for a rail spur and finding a hay distributors; isn't it time we find buyers for the many horses that are ready for sale, to make room for the new ones now arriving." "Bingo, you hit the nail on the head. Zeke tells me we have 72 horses of the old stock ready for riding, cow punching, and light/heavy duty work. The difference in marketing my product is the fact that I have to bring buyers to the ranch since it's not possible to pedal horses to potential buyers all over the country." "So, how do we do it?"

"By holding the first yearly or biyearly 'Circle W Auction.' I want to build a roofed grandstand holding at least 100 customers. In front of stand will be a road leading to a show ring with a stage in the back for the auctioneer. In the show ring, each single horse will have its statistics announced along with any special talents of personal characteristics. The customers will all have a pad to write down the number of each animal or team, and with plenty of room to write down the stats of the animal or team. After a dinner of local beef, we will then hold the auction in the afternoon. Each animal or team will again be brought up for bidding, but to prevent low bids, each animal or team will have a minimum bid. If the minimum bid is not reached, the auction will fail, but the animal will be offered to the bidders for the listed minimum.

If no one accepts it, then the animal goes back in the pasture for the next auction."

"That's a fantastic idea, and we'll do very well financially. So how do you get customers to attend an all-day event and who is responsible for the animal transport?" "Answering your second question first, this is a cash on the barrel sale. The buyer will be responsible for making his own arrangements, and pay the train fees. Our workers will deliver them to the railroad stock yards, and that is where our responsibility will end."

"Now the other question is how to advertise the event and get customers looking to buy horses. After thinking about this one for a while, I'm looking for livery men, large ranchers, groups of small ranchers, freighters, land cultivators, light duty wagon and buggy manufacturers, a myriad of young entrepreneurs looking to start a horse ranch, and many others that don't come to mind. And of course, all these in the major areas to include: Dallas, Austin, New Braunsfeld, San Antonio and Houston."

"Ok, I give up. How on earth can you reach all those people?" "By placing newspaper advertisements in all the local papers. Our own editor at the Waco Times will design a universal advertisement and print out the ad to be sent out. He told me it would include 30 newspapers to run the ad in three daily issues for two weeks or three weekly printings, and would cost an estimated $200."

"What other costs can we expect?" I asked Paul Hall, the construction cost is $125 for the roofed grandstand, $50 for the roof over the show ring and 50 for the roofed auctioneer stage/podium. The meal, using two of our own beefs, is probably another $100. I was thinking of holding the event after the second crop and we could display samples of the two crops—for potential sale."

"Am I allowed to add my thoughts? "Of course, you are my husband and I always hold your ideas highly." "Great, you have the potential of making a memorable event—but not all in one day. Let's make this a two- day event. Instead of parading the animals before noon, the first day will be an open house for anyone to go thru the barns, hay sheds, blacksmith and harness shops, pastures, paddocks and check out the 72 horses you will put up at the auction. Give the buyers time to check out the spec sheets themselves and examine the horses and the harnesses at their pace. You get better bidding when buyers decide they want certain animals before the auction starts—rule 101 of auction sales. Day one starts at 10AM till 4PM and they get a beef burger for the noon meal. Day two starts at 9AM for coffee and registration for a bidding number. The auction starts at 10AM till the noon dinner of meatloaf et al, and continues at 1PM till done. For people who cannot come for the first day, they can make it in one day if they come at daybreak to check out the horses before registration."

"Fantastic, you are a genius. I like your two-day plan." "So who is going to be our auctioneer; it should be someone who knows the animals!" "The one and only deep baritone voice that emits knowledge and authority; Wes Stubridge, my bodyguard, silly!" Branch's eyebrows lifted up as he adds, "of course, hiding in our midst all this time." "Do you think he will accept the job?" "I've already asked him, and he said he would be honored to act as the ranch's representative." "Really, and how many workers know of your idea." "Gary, Zeke, Zeb, Stu, Paul Hall, and the Waco Times editor—the ones that I will rely on to make this happen. Gary is the clerk of the works, Zeke will be in charge of moving the horses, Zeb will feed up to 125 people twice, and Stu is the auctioneer."

After a fabulous meal, the Duo walked over to the warehouse and office of Hofstetter Distributors. Stepping to the customer service window, Branch said, "my wife and I are from Waco and we are crop growers. We have hay to sell and would like to speak to Mister Hofstetter." "Yes, I can smell it, may I see the bag?" The lady receptionist opened the bag and said, "oh my, my! Please follow me."

Walking in Waldo's office she opened the carpetbag and plopped it on Waldo's desk without saying a word. Waldo looked in, smelled the freshness and said, "Mercy mother, is this manna from the heavens?" "Make a deal, or I'm divorcing you," as the lady turns around with a big grin on her face.

My name is Waldo Hofstetter and that was my wife Izzy. We are both of German descent and you are?" "Branch and Gail West of the Circle W ranch in Waco." "Please tell me about your ranch and the crops you are raising."

Waldo was somewhat listening but all he really heard was 400 tons of a triple hay crop, a single crop of +-100-150 tons of straw, and an unknown number of 100-pound bags of oats. Waldo was first to speak, "I can handle, without limits, any amount you can send me. Can you be more specific in estimates?" "Certainly, at this time, we have 200 acres of hay which will yield 400+ tons, and 50 acres of straw which will yield 50 tons of baled straw. For hay, we keep 100 tons, sell 100 tons to our neighbors and you can have the balance of 200+ tons. We have 25 tons of left-over straw from last season that you can have. We will also have a windfall of 100 acres of straw from the seeding of 100 acres now being tilled and you can have most of that harvest. Next year we will have added another 100 acres to our crop lands and will divide the 350 acres into 300 acres of hay and 50 acres of straw."

"How can you guarantee all that when we are expecting a summer drought?" "Because, as we speak, our cropboys are flooding the crop fields and grazing pastures, and we repeat that every 2-3 days." "Really, that is amazing. What would be my cost per ton delivered to Austin?"

"My wholesale price is based on quality, supply and demand. There is always a demand, the quality is guaranteed in all three crops, and my supply to you is guaranteed as you are my only customer. We would like $30 a ton for hay, $20 a ton for straw, and 100-pound bags of oats, or three bushels, at $1.50 per bushel—plus you pay the railroad freight. As soon as the second crop is harvested, I will send you four boxcars— two cars of hay totaling 50 tons, one 25 ton car of straw, and one car of two hundred fifty100-pound bags of oats worth $4.50 per bag"

Waldo looked at the hay sample, smelled it again and said, "you folks are clearly secure with your offer, I won't haggle with you. I'll pay it and it's a deal. How much deposit do you want." "For the first load, the full $3,125, and a contract for this year. For future loads, we'll bill you after you receive it." "How do you know I won't stiff you?" Gail asks, "are you crooked?" Izzy who was listening behind the door, walked in and said, "no he isn't. Waldo, you know this is a good deal, so pay them what they want and give them a contract." "But dear, that's over $3.000!" "So what's the big deal, you have a lot more than that in operational funds. If they come up short, the balance will be applied to next year, I'm sure."

Walking out in good terms, the Duo opened an account in the Austin Wells Fargo branch and deposited the Hofstetter draft. They paid the 1% fee to do a wire transfer to their Wells Fargo branch in Waco. Gail placed their contract in her reticule and pulled out the train schedule. "We can take the evening train home, or we stay in a hotel and go to the theater." "We've done such good business, let's stay over and celebrate. It's still early so let's register in the best hotel and leave our bags. Then, let's go to the racetrack and snoop around and see when the next big race is, heh?"

The racetrack was the similar size as the one in Dallas but the track itself was in better condition. The schedule said that the next monthly race would be held in four weeks, right after completion of the second crop. As they were about to leave a dandy came up to them and said, "you're new here, may I help you?" "Yes, we have Quarter horses that we would like to race in four weeks." "Well, we have limited entries, so if you register now, I can guarantee your horses will all get a chance to qualify and historically, if a horse qualifies at 21 seconds per ¼ mile, it will get to race." So the Duo registered their names and the names of four horses, Wildfire, Sidewinder, Blondie, and Red.

That evening, they changed into city duds and had dinner at the Red Ruby dining room. This was a Victorian restaurant with ragtime piano music, men wearing their fancy Colts and holster rigs, and the ladies wearing low cut dresses with freedom of cleavage. Branch said, "this type of restaurant décor will become a historic landmark, will be upgraded over the years, and 100 years from now, you'll be able to walk in here and walk right in the past."

After a fine seven course meal with prime rib as the main entrée, the Duo took a carriage to the White Theatre and watched a comedic review. On their way home, the carriage driver suddenly pulled up the reins and came to an abrupt stop. A man on foot yells out, "hold it folks, this is a robbery. All I want is your money and I'll be gone." The driver gave him his satchel full of fees, Branch handed him his wallet although he was very tempted to pull out his Bulldog instead. Gail put her hand in her reticule and said, "I only have my coin purse." "Put it in my hand anyways little lady." As Gail complied, the robber's eyes popped out as he saw the lady place her derringer onto his hand and fired. The bullet hit the base of the robber's thumb, amputated it and half of his wrist, and by self- preservation, he collapsed to the ground. Branch jumped off the carriage to grab the thief's Colt, collected his wallet and the driver's satchel. Afterwards, he said to the would-be thief, "you were lucky tonight, the wife usually shoots an attacker's tally-wacker and turns it into a 'tweeter.'" After clearing the shooting with authorities, the Duo left.

That night, Branch kept laughing while reliving the theatre's performance. She was ready and Branch wasn't rising to the occasion, so she decided to take matters in her own hands. It didn't take long for Branch to realize what was on Gail's mind. Finally after a few hours' sleep, the Duo was awake and looking for a replenishing breakfast. They then took the train back to Waco.

*

For the next three weeks till the second crop's harvest, construction was in full swing. Four projects had the finishing touches added. These included the implement drive-thru shed, the Senior West's home, the new bunkhouse, and the expanded baling platform. Afterwards, the Hall carpenters started building Gail's grandstand and stage/podium as well as the Irving's new house and barn. It was a memorable evening when Toby and Jane came to announce that they were expecting their first child. Branch shocked everyone by saying, "well, we'll have Paul start building your new house—of course if you're willing to stay on the ranch?" Before waiting for an answer, he asked, "how many bedrooms would you like?" Jane said, "one downstairs and three upstairs." Gail picked up and said, "sounds like you are planning to stay a while, heh?" Toby answered, "not to say always or never, but this could easily be our permanent home. We are very happy with the work, the coworkers and the pay. Thank You."

Gail was busy supervising the workers in building her grandstand. It was Paul Hall himself who suggested increasing the size to 125 seats since he predicted this would be a popular event with big time buyers within a hundred miles. Zeke also impressed Gail and Paul that a covered shed was needed to keep saddled and harnessed horses out of the sun or rain. Day to day the structure came to life, and Branch was first to give his seal of approval.

The local newspaper editor had prepared a block ad that said,

---

FIRST ANNUAL QUARTER HORSE AUCTION
West Ranch—formerly the
Woods ranch. Waco Tx.
Riding horses and cattle cutting horses,
Harnessed light duty geldings.
Harnessed heavy duty draft Belgians
Private all-day viewing July 29, 1892
(free coffee and noon dinner)

Auction day July 30,1892
Free bidding registration 9AM
Riding and cutting horses 10AM to 12:30PM
Dinner 12:30PM to 1:30PM (FREE)
Light duty harness horses 1:30PM
Medium duty work geldings 2:30PM
Heavy duty Belgian draft horses 3:30PM

NOTE: This is a cash auction but will accept a certified bank draft from the Wells Fargo

Bank of Waco. RSVP by telegram if planning to attend.

Two weeks before the second harvest started, the block ad was sent to the selected newspapers. In preparation for the auction, all the ranch year- round workers were in full swing training horses. Even the farrier, harness maker, Stu, Toby, Gary, Winn, Randy and all the ladies were helping out the trainers. Retrospectively, it was a good thing that Branch had replaced the year-round ranch hands with seasonal workers for the second harvest.

Meanwhile, Branch spent the next weeks watching the railroad workers lay out track. He directed the two side rails to be adjacent to the baling platform. The mobile steam powered conveyor belt could then reach the boxcars or the hay sheds. Once the side rails were completed, Branch requested the delivery of three boxcars to fulfill Hofstetter's first delivery. The arrival of the three boxcars marked the beginning of the second crop harvest.

When the mowers went to work, Gary had to pull back from helping trainers. Now, he and Branch were teaching the seasonal workers to become cropboys. Fortunately, most of these seasonals were experienced homesteaders who needed the supplemental income until their crops came in. On the last day of training, Gary came up to the Duo with a dilemma on his hands. "Four of the seasonals refuse pay. They say they want to repay your loan. Do you know what they are talking about? Gail said, "OOPS. You'd better explain and decide how to handle this, dear?"

Branch explained about the Benefactor Fund and asked him to privately say to all four homesteaders, "if Sam Washburn gave you this money, it was because you needed the help. It was a gift and not a loan. No payback is necessary. So make sure they get equal pay for their work."

When the first wagon full of hay arrived, the wheels went into motion without a hitch. The seasonal workers were on the baling platform and that is where they would stay throughout the harvest as the year-round cropboys were in the field processing the hay and delivering it to the platform. Day after day, now with two full 8-hour shifts the two bailers put out 20 bales of hay per hour equal to +-320 bales per day, or +- 6.5 tons a day.

At the end of the first week, the Duo met with Gary and said, "you mentioned some time ago that next year with another extra 100 acres, that we would need a third baler. It also meant some doubling of a few harvesting implements and more seasonal workers. Order what it takes and make it happen. The baling platform has already been enlarged, and we'd like to run three balers for the third hay crop and the fall oats crop. That way we'll know what is needed for next year." "That's a fantastic idea and I'll order the implements today and find more workers after the second crop harvest."

The harvesting continued and the regular ranch workers were a common finding on the second shift making overtime play money for the coming race in Austin. As soon as the last bale of hay came out of the baler, Zeb had a festive supper prepared in appreciation for a job well done. Over the next day, the workers loaded the three 25-ton boxcars. One for 1st crop hay, one for 2nd crop hay and one for last year's straw.

*

The weekend for the race finally arrived. As a harvest bonus, all workers were given a two-way train ticket to the races in Austin. It also included a day's pay while in Austin. The Circle W workers boarded the train and occupied and entire passenger car. It was a jovial three-hour ride to Austin with music, singing, jokes and even comedy skits. Gail remarked how it was pleasant to see 25+ workers get along this well. Branch responded, 'it's all about a good pay, good meals, decent sleeping quarters, satisfying work, and agreeable workers, heh?" "For sure!"

The train arrived two hours before the race started. Some workers went to a saloon for a few drinks, but most walked amongst the horses to decide the likely horse flesh to win. When the qualifying trials started, many a horse were either a surprised failure or a sleeper racer. When all the chosen horses were matched, the betting started. Each horse had odds to pay if a winner. This was a race where the winning horse paid out the published odds and the looser got nothing.

Betting opened for an hour before the first race and would continue till the beginning of each race. There were six races in the first wave. The winners were then raced again against a second string of fresh horses. So out of 18 horses, six would be eliminated on the first wave. The first wave odds posted on the Circle W Ranch were: Wildfire 1:4, Blondie 1:6, Sidewinder 1:6, and Red 1:12. Gail asked, "why such high odds for Red?" Toby answered. "because they expect her to lose." "Toby do you feel the same?" "Heck no. Both Blondie and Red have finally found their stride and have now surpassed Belle and Lady that we raced in Dallas. Branch met with Stu and arranged the ranch's bets on each of their own horses that had qualified for the first wave.

The first six races were a total win for Circle W. Every one of their four horses won their own race. Sidewinder had won by a nose and Toby suspected something was wrong. After checking him, he found a low- grade fever. Toby then suggested that people bet on the competing horse to win or disqualify Sidewinder. Branch elected to pull him out of the race. So this left the two mares and Wildfire for the second and final wave plus competition from the three other winners.

The odds were then posted for the second wave. Their three horses were given high odds (1:8) since they were expected to be low on energy after their first race. The other horses were all given low odds since they were expected to be the winners. Branch sent Stu to make the bets, and the races began. The West horses won their own races to everyone's surprise.

After the races were over a man tapped Branch on the shoulder. "Sir, my stallion won both his races as your stallion won both of his. What do you say we race them against each other, and the winner gets $5,000 from the looser. Branch looked at the man and said, "I saw you last month at the Dallas races. Why do you look so familiar?" "Because you caused

my brother to hang. My name is Daryl Sutton."
"Oh yes, the human trafficker in Dallas. Very well, the racing bank holds our $5,000 and the winner takes all in a ½ mile race with one turn."

Private bets were being laid down. And of course, the ranch workers were placing their aggressive bets on Wildfire to win. Once betting ceased, the two horses were brought to the starting line. Branch's stallion was a chestnut and Sutton's horse was jet black. Sutton's horse was trying to bite or kick Branch's horse, so the officials separated them by six feet. Branch talked to Randy and warned him to keep a safe distance. The coin toss went for Randy and Wildfire took his place on the left. Even from six feet, the black stallion was still trying to bite Wildfire. Finally, the officials warned that if either horse bit the other during the race that the horse would be disqualified. Sutton tried to defend the fact that racing two stallions was a natural reaction, the officials stood by their decision and let the warning stand.

Tensions were already building as the starting shot rang out, and both horses took off like they had been launched out of a cannon. They were neck to neck, but as they approached the turning post, Sutton's jockey reined his horse closer to Wildfire to make the turn. To everyone's surprise, Sutton horse bit Wildfire in the neck, but because of the distraction to bite, Sutton's horse overshot the post and lost two horse lengths. The race continued but Sutton's horse never corrected the loss and clearly came in second. The crowd went into an uproar. The officials came to examine Wildfire's nipping and proclaimed Wildfire the actual winner and the additional disqualification included a two-year racing suspension for Sutton's horse.

After the race, some ranch workers went to celebrate in the many saloons while others went to find a diner for supper before returning home. Waiting for their meal everyone counted their earnings. The Irvings made $1000 and the Ashburn's made $1,200. Stu was laughing and wouldn't say how he had done. Gail finally said, "we had made $5,000 from the several races, then you bet it all on the race against Sutton and turned it into $10,000. That was a big gamble wasn't it?" "Not really, since Toby had given me the nod while Sutton was talking to me." "How much did you give Randy and Winn for jockey fees? "$200 and $100."

The train ride home was another festive event. The Duo participated but in the back of their minds, they were preparing for the big auction festivities that should place the ranch on the map and become a regular recurring event.

***

CHAPTER 13

The Auction Festivities

Life on the ranch took on a new twist. All the workers realized that their talents and hard work was to be put out for all to criticize or praise. This raised everyone's anxiety to the point that the Duo finally asked the old timers, Zeke and Zeb, what was up with everyone. Zeke started, "I know all the workers and they have extreme pride in their work. In the past they only had to satisfy one customer face to face, now with the auction, they are facing hundreds of scrutinizing eyes." "Zeb added, "now, if you were Obadiah or Benny, how would you like to see one of the saddle broke horse come out to the grandstand bucking the rider off, or be

Ansel or Jane and see a harnessed horse kick at the wagon trying to throw the harness or refuse to follow commands." Gail said, "now I know that is not likely to happen, but the thought of it occurring can certainly get a trainer off his game or cause some sleepless nights. I will address the issue at breakfast tomorrow."

As promised, Gail called a short meeting after breakfast and went right into the issue at hand, "it has come to my attention that several of the ranch workers are getting a bit uptight about the upcoming auction festivities. Notice I called it an 'auction and festivities.' That means you are supposed to be enjoying these two days. You have been preparing these horses for a whole year, and have faith that they will perform as expected. After the event is over, you'll appreciate the opportunity you had to show off your work. For now Zeke will be in charge of moving animals around, Gary will be the clerk of the works, and Stu will be your auctioneer. All three will start preparing you for your individual jobs during the two-day event. All the cropboys will also work as your helpers. I also plan to work with you in the harness division as Branch will be the official greeter. Most important of all, have a good time!"

The weekend before the festivities, the senior Wests arrived with several wagon loads of new furniture and plenty of vittles to fill the larder. The Washburn Mercantile had ordered the furnishings and kept them in storage till Alden and Flora arrived. The entire weekend was spent with the new Wests. Once they informed them of the coming festivities, Flora said she would help Annette and Zeb in the kitchen, and Alden said he would find work helping anyone. They would use this time to get to know all the workers, including the cropboys.

Monday morning arrived and everyone knew they had four days of prep work to be ready for the Friday "show and tell" day. Josh Martin arrived at breakfast time to deliver a box full of telegrams. He added, "I've been collecting these all week. It comes to 50 telegrams acknowledging that a buyer with a wife or foreman or both would attend. The grand total is about 115 attendees so far. I figured that Zeb would want to know as early as possible." "Well thank you Josh, but we'll tell Zeb to prepare for 150 guests and 25 workers to be safe."

The first job was to put away the farm implements and move all the regular cropboys to the teams organizing the festivities. All the barns were emptied of horses to allow Oscar to clean both barns. Once accomplished, the 72 for sale horses were brought inside. The cropboys were assigned the job of brushing and cleaning the animals' coat as well as combing the manes and tails.

The carpenters were busy putting up banners and flags. They crafted a huge sign depicting "The Circle W Ranch," and hung it from the stage's roof. The holding shed needed railings to tie horses. A double row along the right and left side was added. A road was graded leading to the grandstand, then widened between the stage and grandstand, finally returning back to the barns. This allowed horses to be displayed in full view in front of the grandstand—walking in and out without turning back.

Jane and all the trainers kept reviewing commands with all the horses as well as saddling horses to make sure they were not reacting negatively to a rider onboard. Barney spent all four days adjusting harnesses since some of the horses had either grown or gained weight. Buck checked all horseshoes to adjust shoes that had become loose or reshod those that needed it. The wagons used to show harnessed horses were all cleaned up and repainted if needed.

When everything was ready, the Duo, Zeke, Gary and Stu walked around each horse and placed a numbered card to the horse's head gear. On the clipboard, a minimum price was agreed upon for each horse and the 72 listed prices were given to Stu to terminate an auction if the minimum price was not reached.

Friday morning arrived and people started arriving at 7AM from every direction but especially so from the hotels in Waco. The would-be bidders were encouraged to check all the animals, write notes and ask any question about the horses to those in attendance. Ansel described how one customer checked out the horse by touch and appearance. He then checked the teeth, the hooves, the shoes and the quality of the harness hooked on the wall. Then came the questions on age, the stallion and mares as lineage, habits, likes, appetite, friendliness and whether a harnessed horse could also be saddled and ridden. People's finnicky questions amazed everyone, but it certainly simplified Stu's work during the auction. It was clear that bidders would be more aggressive when they had already decided which animal they wanted.

By the noon dinner, some 100 customers were present for a meatloaf, mashed potato, and fresh string bean meal with homemade bread. A white cake finished the meal with plenty of coffee and tea. The afternoon was again busy with throngs of customers examining the different classes of horses. Branch thought it was strange that buyers looking at riding horses were not looking at cowhorses or harnessed horses. Gail pointed out, "Look at that gentleman with a white hat and black vest. He owns a freighting company and he's not interested in anything less than heavy duty geldings or draft Belgians. Now look at that lady in a blue riding skirt, she owns a riding stable in town, and she's only interested in riding mares and geldings."

By the end of the day, most customers agreed to register for the auction. Each was given a bidding card with their own number, and a page of facts to review before the auction:

1. All the horses for sale today are 2 ½--4 ½ years old, and all shod.
2. All horses have been trained for a minimum of 20 commands which are listed below.
3. Riding horses are saddle broke at an early age. We do not use bronc-busting methods.
4. Cow cutting horses are proven in the field.
5. Harnessed horses are fitted with their own harness and is available for purchase after the auctions. Prices are based on the harness's size and total weight. All these horses are saddle friendly.
6. We do not sell saddles, but all our horses come with a bridle/bit or a hackamore.
7. You bid by lifting up your bidding card. Once the bidding appears to come to an end, the auctioneer will say 'going once,

going twice followed by a pause and the word SOLD. Bidding can continue or restart till the word SOLD is clearly heard. Then the auction is closed.

8. All our horses have a registered minimal bid. If the horse minimum bid is not reached, the auctioneer will close the auction and offer the horse to anyone who would pay the minimum. If no one buys it, then the horse goes back to the barn unsold.

9. Our horses come with a no BS guarantee. If you are not satisfied with the horse, we will offer you a replacement or a 100% refund.

At supper, everyone was pleased with the way the day had hashed out. Everyone agreed that very few potential bidders were dissatisfied with the quality of horse flesh being presented. Several potential customers were a bit leery that the hype of the moment bidding against other bidders may jack the values up, but all agreed that the horse quality was top notch.

The Duo was up at dawn. One day buyers were already arriving to check out the horses. Branch started greeting buyers before sunup. By 9AM the ranch grounds were swarming with people. Coffee was served with powdered sugar-coated bearpaws and late comers were registered. At 9:30 a loud 10-gauge shotgun blast invited all present to take a seat in the grandstand.

Stu started once people were sitting down, "welcome to the Circle W for its first annual auction. My name is Wes Stubridge aka Stu. I will represent the ranch as a worker turned auctioneer. To start, please stand for the Pledge Allegiance to the Flag—everyone stands at some form of attention and……..I pledge………..and justice for all."

"To start the festivities, we have a parade of horses that are not for sale. First on our racing stallions Wildfire and Sidewinder are the owners Branch and Gail (Woods) West. Next are our two racing mares with our two jockeys Randy Martin and Winn Stevens, and following them are our two other racing mares with our racing trainer Toby Irving and our horse caretaker Oscar Sands. The next section are our working horses in the crop lands. The first team consists of some gentle beasts weighing 2000 pounds each. They are Belgian draft horses that are the largest horses on the ranch. And last, are our cropboys leading all the work geldings and draft horses we use day to day. As I presume you have noticed, we only have horses with a choice of three coats—Sorrel, Chestnut, and Bay."

Now let's begin with the first category— riding mares. The first is a 3-year old gentle bay ready for riding. She weighs 800 pounds, and her lineage shows the average weight at 1000 pounds. Her characteristics are.......... and who will start the bidding at $125. Gail poked Branch when the lady in a blue riding skirt started the bidding. Three people were bidding at $5 increments. At one point, that lady was so determined to get that horse that she bid twice in a row and the placed broke out in laughter. Well, she finally went for $180 and Stu noted that it was $45 over the minimum as he entered the selling price. Stu then sold the other nine riding mares and noted that the same blue skirt lady had purchased five in all. Also, all nine sold at least $25 above the minimums.

Next were ten riding geldings which sold fast and all above the minimum by at least $30. Most of these were bought by full size men who needed solid mounts. The ten cow cutting horses were all young at 2 ½ years and medium size mares and geldings. They all sold close to the minimum except for one, but it sold when the highest bidder realized he was only $5 below the minimum. And so by noon, thirty horses were sold for a grand total of $4,950.

The noon meal was an extravaganza. Zeb along with Annette and Flora had prepared 125 lbs of potatoes, 75 pounds of carrots, five gallons of beef gravy, baked 25 breads, and as a backup, 25 pounds of leftover meatloaf from yesterday. The main course was beef. A choice of steaks, filet mignon, oven baked beef roast, beef vegetable stew, burgers, and a full hind quarter sliced to your desired thickness. The Duo and the Irvings helped with serving the many choices, along with Zeb, Annette and Flora. Dessert was bread pudding along with the usual coffee and tea.

When everyone was served, there was nothing left in beef. Zeb said this crowd went thru two 2-year old steers. For seconds, to satisfy big eaters, the 25 pounds of meatloaf with left over potatoes and carrots were served till gone. Dessert was very popular and after a long wait, the crowd walked over to the grandstand for the auction's second half.

While they were setting up, Stu mentioned that he had checked the registrations and found that 70% of registrants were here for harness horses. The talk over dinner was that homesteaders were buying modern implements that needed stronger and larger horses. Crop farms were beginning to show up around the state that required horses no smaller than 1,200 pounds. All in all, heavy bidding was expected, and every purchase would likely include the horse's fitted harness.

Welcome back we will start with the light duty harnessed horses for buggies and buckboards. We have 7 for sale. The bidding started and wives seemed to edge their husbands on. Whether it was the low number of beautiful horses, or some other factors, each went $40 over the minimum and the harnesses went for $125.

The next category was medium duty geldings to pull single blade plows and most homesteading functions including light duty farm wagons. The ten went quickly and the buyers were clearly independent homesteaders. The harnesses sold for $150.

When it got to the heavy-duty geldings and draft horses, Stu pointed out that these were all 4+year olds. The geldings were all +-1300 pounds, and the draft horses were +-1500 pounds. The bidding started and it was a battle between freighters and homesteaders wanting to use modern implements. The 15 heavy duty geldings went for an average of $250 each and the draft Belgians went for an outlandish $350 each. The gelding harnesses sold for $175 and the draft horse harnesses sold for $250.

After the last horse was sold, Gail made a sign to Stu to hold the crowd in the stands as she spoke to Branch. "The sale's total is almost $23,000." "What? That's not an embarrassment, it's highway robbery, what do you suggest?" "Well our minimum bids would have yielded a total of $16,000. So why don't we give everyone a 10% discount on the winning price for the horses, not for the harnesses that are priced to cover labor and parts." "Agree." "Then I believe you should make the announcement yourself, heh? "Ok." Branch walks to the podium and starts, "Gail and I appreciate your attendance and vigorous bidding. But at an auction, a bidder has a competitive incentive because someone is bidding against him. Normally this is good news for the owners, but the response today was way above the line. We don't want anyone to go home and say, 'I got a superior animal, but I paid up the nose for it, I am not going to that auction again.' So, to make things more equitable, anyone who bought a horse today can deduct 10% off the purchase price."

The only thing that could be heard was 150 people breathing in and out, then realty set in and the place roared to life with guffaws, whistles, and applause. People started to step to the office at the ranch house to pay for their purchase. Gail was taking the cash or the certified bank draft from the Wells Fargo Bank in Waco. Present at the payoff was the bank president who would certify the bank drafts. The head railroad agent was also present to make arrangements for horse and harness transfer to their destination. By 6PM, the Duo was sitting on the porch, each with a cold bottle of Doctor Pepper and totally exhausted. Branch said, "Zeb is making a light supper of an omelet with bacon, cheese, and onions. What do you say we go to supper and then go to bed to get some sleep?" "And skip extracurricular activities?" "Yes?" "Ok."

*

The next morning, after making up lost extracurriculars, the Duo had a replenishing breakfast, then with an armed guard of Stu, Gary, Zeke and Ansel, the Duo brought $10,000 in cash and $10,000+ in bank drafts to the Wells Fargo Bank in town. Before going back home, the Duo went around town paying off creditors. On their way back home, Branch asked what Gail's goals were for the next year. "Well the auction brings all the workers back to a regular schedule. Guess I'm just going to supervise activities and help out where I can. I love the horse business and that's what I want to continue doing. I'm happy with the recent additions, but the yearly foals from now on will add 100 horses a year, and that's enough to maintain my herd of +- 300 horses." "What about you?"

"I want to get more involved with crop farming. We are getting a bunch of new implements and a third baler. The cropboys have the 100 acres of new land ready for planting an oats crop as is the regular 50 acres already planted. By doing this, we will have a minimum of 350 acres of hay to harvest next year, drought or no drought. I am seriously thinking of pushing the envelope and cultivating some more land this fall and winter to get ready for hay spring planting. There is a market out there to supply cattle ranchers who fight drought or heavy winter kill from deep snow. With the trains, our crops can reach anywhere out west. So I see my destiny finally."

"That's your current goal, but what is your long-term goal?" "I want to build a forage crop growing empire and start adding alfalfa to hay and oats. Beyond that, I want to become a grain producer by planting corn, soybeans, sorghum, and barley, along with the regular oats. This means building silos to store the grains and buying special harvesting implements. We have the perfect weather and are well situated in central east Texas. Starting tomorrow, I plan to take over the crop business and move Gary to your side for horse raising and training. I guess I'm getting ahead of things, aren't I?"

"Wow, you are all fired up aren't you. I see stability in my ranch, and you see an opportunity to grow an empire. If this is your destiny, then enjoy it. We have the funds and the land to expand. Don't hold back. So what do we do about our marshal status?" "I heard that Waco is getting a new marshal to work with PF and Pappy, so we'll turn in our badges and resign." "Are you sure?" "Woman, I am so happy with you and our lives that I am busting at the seams to say so. We're not living by the gun anymore. And that's my story, but make sure I stick to it"

Well, I think this is the time to fess up, even if we are on a buggy going 3mph. You see I have a secret, and sending me to town with a bodyguard is not the best way to keep a secret. So Stu is threatening to tell if I don't speak up before the third harvest. Doctor Ross said I was with child and I love you." Branch pulled the reins and turned to look at his wife in total shock. His mouth was open, but he was speechless. "Yes, we're going to be parents and fill that house with kids." "The best of news, and I love you too! Family is a lot more important than business and will be our shared destiny. Thank you for providing the ultimate gift."

The Duo was silent, thinking things over. It was Gail who said, "we are so blessed: we have a great home, we are in love, we have each our day to day work activities, and we are finally blessed to have children."

"As I said, this is the American dream and a destiny worth cherishing, heh?" "For sure!"

***

The End